D0051544

Trish Morey

THE ITALIAN BOSS'S SECRET CHILD

EXPECTING!

HARLEQUIN®
Live the emotion™

www.eHarlequin.com
HARLEQUIN PRESENTS®

ISBN 0-373-12486-4

9 780373 124862

50450

S EAN

"I'm carrying your child."

"This is ridiculous," he said. "We've never even had sex. The only time we came anywhere near close was at the Gold Coast, and you threw me out of your room before I had hardly a chance to kiss you. Remember? So if you're pregnant from that time, someone else must be the father."

"You really must have a pretty low opinion of me if you think I'm capable of falling into bed with any guy who crosses my path."

"Well…" He pointedly gazed at her lower abdomen. "Given your condition, you've obviously fallen into bed with somebody."

"Maybe not," she said, a smile emerging at her lips for the first time in their conversation. "Who said this baby had anything to do with bed?"

"What the hell is that supposed to mean?"

She looked right at him, desperate to take the smug look off his face. "The office Christmas party. Tell me, exactly how many women *did* you make love to in the boardroom that night?"

Relax and enjoy our fabulous series about
couples whose passion ends in pregnancies...
sometimes unexpected!
Of course, the birth of a baby is always a
joyful event, and we can guarantee that our
characters will become wonderful moms
and dads—but what happened in
those nine months before?

Share the surprises, emotions, drama and
suspense as our parents-to-be come to terms
with the prospect of bringing a new baby
into the world. All will discover that the
business of making babies brings with it
the most special love of all....

Delivered only by Harlequin Presents®

Trish Morey

THE ITALIAN BOSS'S
SECRET CHILD

EXPECTING!

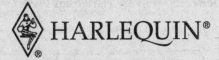

HARLEQUIN®

TORONTO • NEW YORK • LONDON
AMSTERDAM • PARIS • SYDNEY • HAMBURG
STOCKHOLM • ATHENS • TOKYO • MILAN • MADRID
PRAGUE • WARSAW • BUDAPEST • AUCKLAND

ISBN 0-373-12486-4

THE ITALIAN BOSS'S SECRET CHILD

First North American Publication 2005.

CHAPTER ONE

WHAT a day! So far he'd chewed out two suppliers who'd let him down, put the fear of God into his IT guru for delivering late—again—on the new system and had a stand up fight with the HR manager, who seemed to think it was a good idea to pay every single employee a Christmas bonus generous enough to rival the gross national product of any number of tiny Third World nations.

Not yet eleven o'clock and already he'd been through the wars.

Not yet eleven o'clock and already it was shaping up to be the perfect day.

He pushed back in his leather recliner chair until he was almost horizontal, hands clinched behind his neck, legs stretched out with feet on the desk, and breathed deeply. Closing his eyes against the Melbourne skyline shown to full advantage from the floor to ceiling glass windows of his Collins Street office tower, he relived the turbulence of the morning's altercations.

Ruthless, difficult and a man to be feared, Damien DeLuca's reputation as the toughest CEO south of the equator wasn't likely to come under threat today.

Which suited him just fine. He was proud of his reputation—after all, it had taken him long enough to build. As a first generation Australian, the youngest son of Italian parents who'd left everything they'd known to make a new life in Australia over thirty-five years ago, he'd worked hard to get where he was. From humble beginnings helping out in the family's former market garden, he'd made the most of a scholarship to a top college, then followed it up with a successful stint at university. Seven years later he'd walked away with a double degree plus a masters in business and a raft of eager employment offers to select from.

It had given him the start he'd needed. Within two years he'd set up his own financial sector software company and begun making inroads into the same competition that had been so desperate to snap him up.

A few more years on and he'd taken over two of his rivals and was an acknowledged innovator in the industry. Other companies now looked to his for an example of how to succeed. It was hardly a secret. He hadn't built Delucatek by being soft. He'd got where he was by being tough, by expecting a lot from himself and from his staff.

And he'd done it on his own. He had no time for partnerships, no time for sharing control. He was the boss, pure and simple. That was the way he ran his life, in the boardroom as well as in the bedroom. The women that flitted in and out of the scene were soon made aware of it too, even if they sometimes thought they could change him. They were wrong. He didn't need them.

Damien DeLuca didn't need anyone.

He pulled an arm out from behind his head, flashed a look at his TAG Heuer watch and frowned. Enid Crowley, his PA, should be returning from her break with his coffee any minute. Meanwhile his marketing manager, Sam Morgan, was late for his meeting to present the international marketing proposal to launch Delucatek's newest software package.

Very late!

He swung his legs down off the desk, irritated that someone who needed his approval to splash hundreds of thousands of the firm's dollars on what he understood was a radically different campaign hadn't even bothered to show up yet. It didn't augur well for the proposal.

It augured even less well for Sam.

What a day! She didn't need this. Not today.

Philly Summers hugged the file containing the proposal to her chest, her eyes still itching with the threat of tears, her throat tight and constricted, and knowing that all too soon she'd be deposited at the executive level of the DeLuca Tower whether she liked it or not.

Of all the days for Sam to go down with flu!

In normal circumstances she'd be celebrating being called in at the last minute to present the marketing plan to the famous if feared head of Delucatek. After three months working as Sam's deputy, it was clear to her that he was a man more than happy to take a disproportionate amount of credit for the work of others.

In normal circumstances she'd consider it a real coup, having the chance to present what was ninety-nine per cent her very own proposal to the man who could make or break her career in a moment.

In normal circumstances...

But these weren't normal circumstances.

Today she had more important things to worry

about than where her career might be headed or in seizing opportunities when they came knocking.

She sucked in a deep breath, seeking fortification, but the oxygen charged air was no match for the memory of the words that played over and over again in her mind. ''I'm sorry but legally we can't help you. If you were married...''

If she was married! Now there was a joke. Bryce had well and truly put paid to any chance of that when he walked out two months ago, barely one week before their wedding. Besides which, if she'd been married she wouldn't have had to seek the help of the IVF clinic in the first place—she might already be pregnant.

But she wasn't married.

No man. No prospects. Not a chance of conception unless she considered trawling the late night bars and clubs for a stud. Her teeth dragged a path through her lip-gloss. Would she dare? Was a promise made to a dying woman worth stooping to such levels?

Her mother's pain-racked face flashed in her mind's eye, her once soft features twisted and hardened with both the progress of her disease and the anguish of deep, unbearable loss. She thought she'd do anything to assuage her mother's pain, to give her hope, but could she resort to picking up some no-name one-night stand in order to fulfil her promise?

'No,' she whispered on a shiver, her voice cracking in the empty lift. No question. She might be desperate but reckless wasn't her style. She lifted a hand and swiped at the sudden moisture on her cheek, recognising that maybe it meant there was no way she'd be able to fulfil the promise she'd made.

Maybe she'd just have to accept that she wasn't

going to be able to give her mother the grandchild she craved more than anything—the grandchild she needed to make her smile again. It wasn't fair but maybe it just wasn't going to happen.

The button marked forty-five lit up with a ding, breaking into her thoughts as the door slid open on to the plush foyer of the executive level. She stepped out, fingers white-knuckled on the file as she tried to turn her thoughts back to the proposal. This meeting needn't take long. She could focus on the proposal for the few minutes it would take. She knew it by heart after all, given she'd written just about every word of it.

Then she'd go back to her office and think this whole thing through again. She couldn't give up now—not while there was still time. Based on her mother's prognosis, she still had three months to conceive. Three chances to fulfil her promise. She would come up with something. There had to be another way.

There had to be.

'Sam! You're late. Come right through.'

The voice, deep and edged with impatience, emanated from the open office door adjacent to the unmanned workstation to her left. Dazzling light from the windows beyond illuminated the door, bright and radiant, before splashing into the corridor and bouncing along the walls.

'Sam!'

It had to be him. She'd only spoken to him once and that had been very early on in her three months with the company when she'd answered Sam's unattended phone, but if she wasn't mistaken that was the voice of Delucatek's esteemed and highly feared leader, Damien DeLuca. Admittedly it had been a very brief conversation as Sam had just about wrenched the phone from her ear when he'd discovered who was calling, but she'd lay money on those strident and demanding tones originating from the man everyone quietly and reverently called *Numero Uno*.

She tugged at the hem of her sensible tweed jacket, steeling herself for her meeting with a man coffee room chatter insisted was more to be feared than the Godfather.

'Sam!'

Philly jumped in irritation. Godfather indeed! Just where did this guy get off? He might be her boss and admittedly he might even be a genius where his business was concerned, but she just wasn't in the mood to put up with some egomaniac today. Especially not some shouting egomaniac.

She sucked some air into her lungs and pushed herself down the corridor in the direction of the open office door. The voice beat her to it.

'Well?' the voice rang out again impatiently before someone suddenly dimmed the lights. She blinked and opened her eyes to see the body that owned the voice filling much of the doorway. At least that accounted for the diminution of light—as his broad-shouldered body effectively blocked the dazzling rays. She stopped dead, just paces away, as his backlit form loomed tall and dark over her, his outline glowing like an aura, features indiscernible as her eyes tried to adjust to the sudden shift in the light.

She knew what he looked like, the marketing department had a filing cabinet full of photos of the boss in various poses—working at his desk, leaning over an employee at his computer, standing in the forefront of the building named after him.

She knew what he looked like, from the calculating, sharp eyes topped with thick, dark brows to his rugged, square jaw and the cleft in the centre of his chin. Dark hair backswept to control the strong natural wave and generous classic bow lips. He had features that film stars would envy. Some would have to spend a fortune on cosmetic surgery in an effort to attain the same brooding good looks.

Yes, she knew exactly what he looked like—yet still she felt a *frisson* of sensation shimmy down her spine. None of the photos hinted at what she now felt, at what his shadowed face spoke to her.

Danger.

Excitement.

And maybe, just maybe, something more…

CHAPTER TWO

'WHO are you?'

The woman in the mousy-brown suit seemed to stiffen, her jaw open as if in shock as her eyes searched his face. She clung on to the folder in front of her as if it was body armour and, given the size of her, she could do with it. There was so little to her it looked as though the folder was the only thing anchoring her to the earth.

'You're not Sam,' he accused.

Her mouth snapped shut and her chin kicked up. The action added only millimetres to her tiny frame but by the sudden spark in her eye he got the impression she imagined she was looking straight into his. Then her eyebrows arched and her lips curved into a smile.

Momentarily he relaxed. She wasn't completely mousy, now that she was smiling. In fact, in a way, she was quite pretty—in a homely sort of way. Of course, the tortoiseshell glasses and shapeless brown suit didn't do her any favours.

'Mr DeLuca,' she said, tilting her head to one side, her surprisingly husky voice edged with honey as she relaxed her grip on the folder enough to hold out a hand to him. 'They told me you were a genius. Obviously they were right.'

The way her hazel eyes glinted told him she hadn't just paid him a compliment.

He sucked in a breath, desperate to replace the lungful that had just been knocked out of him, as she kept right on smiling and holding her hand out in the air between them as if she hadn't meant a thing with her last comment.

'I'm Philly Summers, from Marketing. Pleased to meet you.'

He looked at her hand, hanging there, then crossed to the fake smile she was brandishing, and knew she was lying. She was no more pleased to meet him than he was to find Miss Brown Mouse lurking outside his office. What on earth was Sam Morgan thinking to send her? He gave her hand a brief shake, momentarily annoyed that someone so diminutive could have such a firm grip, before he swivelled around and stalked across the floor of his office.

'Where's Sam?' he asked once he'd deposited himself back in his deep leather chair, elbows on arm rests, a Mont Blanc fountain pen spinning between his fingers.

She hesitated for a moment by the door before apparently assuming he'd invited her to follow him, taking a few tentative steps towards the desk.

'Hopefully home by now. He's got the flu. He just about collapsed at his desk half an hour ago. We sent him home in a taxi.'

'And no one thought to inform me?'

Her head tilted to one side again and her eyes narrowed to slits, almost as though she thought he had a nerve asking the question.

'I was led to believe you were informed.'

'I wasn't.'

She considered him for a second, looked for a moment as if she would argue, but then thought better of it.

'In any event I assume it is more important that your presentation goes ahead as planned. I understand you have a very tight schedule and who knows when Sam will be back on deck? And we really need your go-ahead on this proposal today if we're to meet our timelines for the new product launch.'

And her taking the initiative was meant to impress him?

Dammit but it did. Everything she said made sense. So why did he still feel so aggrieved?

Because he should have been told!

He grunted in response, waving to a seat. 'So long as you have some idea of what the proposal is. I don't want to waste my time here.'

The muscles tightened around her mouth as if she'd just had to button it, but she kept on standing. 'I'll do my best not to waste a moment. However, I'll need to access your computer, if you don't mind. I've put a PowerPoint presentation on the share drive we can go through. This hard copy…' she indicated the file in her hands '…is for your records.'

He shrugged and gestured to the laptop on his desk. 'Be my guest,' he said, without moving an inch.

A blink was her only response. *Good.* Did she really expect him to make this easy for her after the lip she'd given him? If she wanted his computer, she could come and get it.

'I'm all ears,' he invited, a smile finally finding its way to his face. At last it looked as if he'd turned the tables on Miss Mouse. He wouldn't be surprised if any moment now she scampered back to her hole in the wall.

He watched her swallow, following the movement in her throat to her chest, which rose on a deep breath, considerably further than he would have expected. But then, with her jacket buttoned up to her neckline, there was no way of saying what lay beneath the uninspiring cut of her suit.

'All right,' she said, rounding the desk until she was on his side. She surveyed his legs, currently providing a very effective barrier between her and easy access to the computer, and almost as if she'd determined they were an immovable object reached over them to the laptop on the far side of his desk. A faint hint of something fruity and sweet stirred his senses as she stretched across him.

He prided himself on knowing the names of all the top perfumes and he had a talent for picking them for his dates. A different perfume for a different skin, a different personality, a different woman. To Carmel, sleek and elegant, he'd given the classic Chanel No.5. Warm and lush, Kandy had adored the heady tones of Opium, while for Belinda, fair and dreamlike, he'd chosen Romance.

But this perfume was something new, totally unlike anything else he'd come across. Something tantalisingly unsophisticated.

It suited her. She sure looked innocent enough. Though the way her skirt hugged her as she stretched over his legs—there was shape hidden away under that skirt after all. She straightened and his nostrils caught a second subtle whiff. *Apricot?* Yeah, she smelled like apricots. That *was* different.

*   *   *

Where did this guy get off? Didn't he realise she was doing him a favour? Next time he could wait for Sam to get back from sick leave. She didn't need this kind of aggravation in her life right now.

She swivelled the laptop around and drew it closer to where she stood so that she didn't have to keep bending over the boss's legs. She could almost feel his eyes boring into her back, searing her skin through her wool mix suit until it prickled, just knowing he was there, a bare metre behind her, scrutinising her every step of the way.

Knowing he was her boss in no way suppressed the sensations she was experiencing right now. *Raw sexuality.* It emanated from him in waves. Even the way he casually sprawled in his chair couldn't hide the latent power contained in those long limbs. She was used to dealing with bosses on equal terms—not one had ever made her so aware of his inherent sexuality.

Not one had made her so aware that he was a man. *That she was a woman.*

She shifted, comfortable with neither where her thoughts were going nor how her body was suddenly tingling. He sure wasn't making this easy. But then, no one had ever described Damien DeLuca as easy.

Impossible; arrogant; genius—she'd heard all those words used in conjunction with his name. But easy? Ha! Not a one. The sooner she got through with this meeting and got out of here the better. If only she could focus on her presentation!

Naturally his sudden appearance at the door had thrown her. Just for a moment there had seemed something more to Damien than she'd heard, another angle, another dimension.

She'd been kidding herself. Now that his face was out of the shadows he was just another good-looking, over-achieving workaholic who had no people skills whatsoever.

She turned her head a fraction and caught a glimpse of his smug-looking face out of the corner of her eye as she manoeuvred her way through explorer to the share drive.

Okay, maybe that wasn't quite fair. Make that drop-dead gorgeous, over-achieving workaholic who lacked people skills but exuded testosterone by the bucketload. *That* might be closer to the mark.

The photos in the marketing files certainly didn't do him justice. No doubt the current photographer had been in place since the year dot. First thing she'd do when she got back to her office would be to organise a new photographer who knew how to use great material rather than take it for granted. Because whatever his personality faults, the guy sure had great genes. No doubt that with his looks and IQ his kids were bound to be intelligent and great looking, just like their dad.

Maybe what she needed was a guy like him?

Her fingers stopped dead over the mouse, her mouth suddenly, inexplicably dry.

Why would that occur to her? Clearly her other problem was starting to affect her brain. Now she was having fantasies about the men at work. Or, at least, fantasies about this one.

And having fantasies about Damien DeLuca was pointless. He was so far out of her league it wasn't funny. Even if he wasn't, from what she'd heard, the guy was a confirmed bachelor—a one man band all the way and probably just as well the way he treated people. You'd have to be mad to get tangled up with someone like him.

Not that getting tangled up with Damien was on the cards.

'Is something wrong?'

She jumped as if she'd been stung. 'Oh, no.' She shook her head, shielding from him what she had no doubt would be a give-away red face. 'Not at all. Um, here's the file…'

She took a couple of steadying breaths before finally turning. With the opening slide on the screen that she hoped would pull attention from her sudden colour, she gave a weak smile. 'Okay, all set?' she asked before launching into her presentation.

'What do you know about her? That *Filly* woman. Though I have to say she looks more like a mouse than any horse I've seen.'

Without looking up from her computer screen or mis-hitting a key on her one hundred words per minute typing speed, Enid responded drily, 'And I should know?'

'You know everything about everyone in this office, Enid, and you know it.'

She still didn't look up, but he did notice the tiniest tweak at the corner of her line-rimmed lips.

'Then it's Philly, with a P-H, short for Philadelphia. Her parents had a travel urge at one time apparently, though never got farther than the maternity unit at Melbourne General.'

'Family?'

'Lives with her mother. A widow. There was a

brother, though he died in tragic circumstances, I believe.'

He raised his eyebrows. 'Anything else?'

'Twenty-seven years old, single—was about to be married a month or two ago but something happened. Could be a left at the altar story.'

Left at the altar? Yeah, that would do it. He'd got the distinct impression that despite her professional presentation she had a real thing against men.

'By the way,' she said, 'now that you've finished early you might like to tackle your messages.' She swivelled around on her chair to pick up a stack of papers she handed over to him. 'Don't worry about the top one; Sam left a brief message on my voicemail while I was out that he was unable to do the presentation. No doubt you got that message anyway.'

He looked briefly at the stack before pocketing them. So Philly had been right. Someone had tried to let him know. So now he couldn't even hold that against her. He wasn't entirely sure he liked that.

'Snippy little thing,' he said as he rested a hip on her desk, putting down his now tepid coffee and replacing it with a card from her in-tray, spinning it between his fingers. 'Did a good job, though—really knows her stuff. Sam would have taken three times as long. But I don't think she likes me.'

'*No one* at Delucatek likes you. You're the original boss from hell and you love it.'

'But you like me, Enid.'

Enid's fingers stopped dead on the keyboard, her index finger hovering pointedly over the ''I''. She looked up at him over her reading glasses, her eyes narrowed to slits, and she let her head tip to the side in a bare nod. 'I have a great deal of respect for you—yes, that's true. In addition to which I have to admit you do wonderful things for my cash flow. But like you?' The movement of her head now looked less of a nod and more of a shake.

He held up his hand before she could say any more. 'Okay.' He laughed, rich and loud. Of course she was kidding. She was crazy about him. 'Why is it you're the only person in this building who doesn't take me seriously?'

'Somebody has to do it,' she replied, adding a wink for good measure before she turned back to her keyboard.

He stopped flipping the card in his hands long enough to read it.

'Damn. Whoever decided on a masked fancy dress theme for this year's Christmas party?'

'*You* did,' came the terse response. 'You said it would help break down barriers between the staff—get them warmed up and mixing without copious quantities of alcohol. And I think it's a great idea.'

'What are you going as, Enid? Little Bo Peep?'

The look she gave him was pure ice and the lines around her pursed lips condensed to form canyons.

'And there I was thinking Xena, Warrior Princess was more my style. Besides,' she continued, 'I'm not telling. You'll have to work it out on the night. Masks only come off at midnight.'

He shrugged. It was a good idea to break the ice. Break down the barriers he could already see developing between his managers and their staff. Barriers were the last thing he wanted and it was clear, if Sam and the Marketing Department were any example, that those barriers were already being put up. He'd had no idea there was someone in that area with the skills Philly possessed—Sam had certainly never mentioned her.

And it would be interesting to see what his staff came up with for their disguises. Some people wouldn't need much help of course. Already he could see Miss Brown Mouse—with the addition of a couple of little pink ears and a tail she'd be utterly convincing.

CHAPTER THREE

'YOU look like a princess!'

Philly smiled and did a twirl as she entered her mother's room, the ends of her black wig flicking out as she spun. 'You don't think it's too much? The woman in the costume shop said it was fine.'

'Too much? No, dear, it's just perfect. You'll be the belle of the ball.'

'I don't know about that.'

'Oh, but I've got some lovely perfume I never wear any more that would be perfect with that outfit.' She pointed the way to the cabinet and Philly followed her directions, giving a spray to her neckline and wrists. It was nice, rich and exotic, and quite a change from her usual apricot scent. Well, tonight was the night for change, or so it seemed.

She plumped the pillows behind her mother's frail back, making sure she was comfortable before fetching her a cup of tea. Then she sat down on the bed alongside and held out a small saucer holding several brightly coloured pills.

'I still don't know why I'm going, really. If you'd prefer, I'm quite happy to stay home.'

'You don't get out enough as it is,' said her mother, her fingers hunting down a fat capsule. 'You should enjoy it when you get the chance.' She dropped the pill on her tongue, washing it down with a swig of tea as she foraged for another.

'I guess going out just doesn't bother me all that much,' she said with a shrug.

'Then it should. It's not natural for a young woman to shut herself away from the world when she should be out there enjoying it and meeting people.'

'I've got a job. I meet plenty of people.'

Her mother took another sip of tea, picking up the last few pills.

'You're not still pining over that Bryce, are you?'

Philly pulled a face in response, putting the now empty dish over on the bedside table. Of course it had hurt, being dumped for another woman like that just before their wedding—another woman she'd discovered he'd been seeing for a year, another woman he'd made pregnant. She'd felt stupid, naïve and desperately hurt. Most of all she'd felt cheated of the child she was so desperate to have, a child he'd so freely given someone else, and for a while she'd longed to have him back. For a while.

'No,' she said on a sigh, knowing it was true. Abandoning her one week before their wedding had come as a huge shock. He'd let her down badly and knocked her confidence for a six but she wasn't exactly without blame over the failure of the relationship herself.

She'd fallen in with his plans for marriage, indeed his plans for everything, because it had suited her to do so. And while she'd believed she loved him, she knew now that she'd talked herself into it because she'd so desperately wanted it to be right, to make forming a family with him and having his child right.

But it hadn't been right. She would have been marrying him for all the wrong reasons.

'Marriage to Bryce would have been a mistake; I

know that now,' she said, squeezing her mother's hand. 'He did us both a favour by walking away when he did.'

Her mother nodded. 'He just wasn't the one for you. But the right man *is* out there, you mark my words. Look at Monty; he took out dozens of girls before he found that one special woman. Annelise was so sweet. They were so happy together.'

Her mother sighed wistfully, and together their gazes drifted to the framed photo standing in pride of place on her dressing table. The smiling couple, beaming their happiness and their pride as together they held up their newborn son for the camera.

It was happiness that had been tragically short-lived. The very next day, on their way to show off the new arrival to his grandmother, all three lives had been wiped out, victims of foul weather conditions and a horrendous light plane crash.

Philly drew in a breath and turned to her mother, still transfixed by the photo and clearly thinking, re-membering, as two tears slid a crooked path down her hollow cheeks. Then her mother sniffed, still looking at the photo.

'I'd just love to see you settled, dear, bef…' Her words trailed off mid-sentence but she didn't have to finish them. Philly knew what she'd been going to say—the unspoken words hung fat and heavy in the air, weighed down with the inevitability of what was to come.

Before I die.

Something squeezed tight in her chest.

Less than twelve months to live. Her mother de-served some happiness, something to look forward to. Something that promised a future that would take her mind and thoughts beyond the doctors' sad prognosis. Something to help her—not forget, she could never forget—but maybe just ease the pain she was feeling at the premature deaths of a young family who'd had everything to live for.

Instead she was giving herself up to the disease, accepting her fate almost as if she was looking forward to being reunited with her late husband and especially Monty, his beautiful wife and the grandchild she knew by this one lone photograph.

The doctors had been sympathetic when the drugs just didn't seem to work any more in arresting the disease. 'She has to want to live,' they'd said. 'People often need something to live for, a reason to survive.'

Philly had failed her. She'd promised to give her mother a grandchild but now, with a failed relationship, an aborted marriage behind her and not even eligible for IVF, she'd run out of options. Sure, there was a chance she might find a boyfriend in that time, but there was no way she was likely to settle down and form a family within the next twelve months— no way she was going to be able to brighten her mother's last few months with the promise of a child.

But then, what real chance did she have of even finding a boyfriend? Every time she'd thought about men or dating lately only one man had sprung to mind. Every guy she met paled in comparison. He was better looking, better built, more intelligent and had a charisma that reeled her in.

She shook her head. Work must really be getting to her if Damien DeLuca kept crowding her thoughts. Sure, he had great genes but if she kept comparing every guy she met with him she was never going to find anyone who made the grade. And she couldn't even say that she liked him—he was far too arrogant and autocratic—though he sure had plenty going for him besides.

What would he be dressed as tonight? Probably a pirate with his looks. A buccaneer, swashbuckling and dangerous, in a soft shirt, ruffled at the sleeves and open over his chest, the stark white a contrast against his dark hair and tanned olive skin, and tucked into tight black breeches...

Her mother tugged a tissue from the box on her bedside table, pulling Philly out of her thoughts with a jolt. Her nervousness at attending this costume ball must be getting to her. Now she was imagining all sorts of strange things.

'Oh dear, I am getting maudlin,' her mother said, blotting away her tears and then blowing her nose. 'Don't listen to me. I'm just tired.'

'You get some sleep then,' Philly said, squeezing the older woman's hand gently and kissing her softly on the cheek before she picked up the empty cup.

'I won't be late.'

She shouldn't have come.

From behind her sequinned mask she took one look inside the door, saw the myriad of characters in the lavishly decorated auditorium, the mirror balls spinning crazy colours against the bizarre outfits of the crowd dancing to the loud music, and knew she should have stayed at home.

What was she doing here anyway?

Standing in the lobby, tossing up whether or not to enter the party, she didn't know. Yes, it had been nice to dress up, to put on something pretty rather than shrug into her sensible work wardrobe for a change—

Lord knows it had been long enough since she'd taken so much care with her appearance. But what did she hope to achieve by it?

Who did she think she was trying to impress— Damien? Fat chance. In terms of being a woman, he didn't know she was alive and he probably didn't even care. The way he'd tried to make her feel so inconsequential when she'd given that presentation… It was pure fantasy to think that she might make an impression on him tonight.

As if he cared.

She wouldn't go in. There was no point at all. Even if she didn't harbour a tiny desire to turn the tables on the one guy who'd made her feel as insignificant as a gnat, she was just no good at this sort of thing. No good at mixing with near strangers. Sure, she'd met plenty of pleasant people in the few short months she'd been at Delucatek, but no one she knew well enough yet to term a friend. Though admittedly that was nobody's fault but her own. She'd been the one to turn down the Friday after work drinks invitations, always too anxious to go home and see to her mother.

And, of course, after Bryce and the fiasco of their wedding, trusting people enough to get close to them hadn't been high on her list of priorities. Just because he'd made the right decision in calling off the wedding didn't mean she'd forgotten the pain of cancelling the church and reception and explaining to the invited guests that the wedding was now off.

The external doors behind her swung open as a new party of guests arrived and the summer night air rushed inside, clashing with the air conditioning in a gust that swirled across her bare shoulders and under her slim-fitting gown. She hugged her arms to her, fighting the unfamiliar sensations as she sidled as inconspicuously as possible out of their path, using a potted palm as a screen.

She must be crazy!

As soon as this group extinguished their cigarettes and entered the party the coast would be clear and she'd make her escape.

'Hello? Who have we here? Don't tell me—Cleopatra. Am I right?'

She looked up at the gruff voice, startled to see a large nun, complete with moustache and cigar, bearing down on her, the eyes of the rest of his group all turned in her direction. The most disturbing thing was that the nun sounded exactly like Sam Morgan.

'Don't you look something! Aren't you Sylvia from Accounts?' He took hold of her hand in his own meaty paw and pulled her out from behind the pot plant where she'd sought refuge.

She looked at them all, speechless. A fluffy grey koala, Tin Man and Humpty Dumpty all stared back.

'Sylvia?' the nun prompted. 'Is that you under that sexy get-up?'

She shook her head, unwilling to give away her identity. If she was going to go home, the last thing she wanted was for Sam to question her on Monday as to her sudden disappearance. She'd rather people thought she'd never bothered to attend. 'Um. Marie,' she murmured, trying to add a different note to her voice. 'From—the Sydney office.'

'Welcome, Marie!' said the nun. 'No wonder you're shy. Why don't you come in with us? We'll take good care of you. Won't we, Tin Man?'

Tin Man rattled as he tried to nod enthusiastically, earning himself a quick dig in the ribs from the koala.

Before she could protest and extricate her hand from Sam's, Humpty grabbed her other one and together they steered her towards the doors. 'Don't worry about Tin Man and Koala,' Humpty said conspiratorially. 'Newlyweds. And I know we're not supposed to take off our masks till midnight, but I'm Julia. If you get lost or need any help, look for Sister Sam—' she nodded her big egg head in the direction of the nun '—or me. Now, let's join the party, shall we?'

Before Philly could protest, she'd been swept into the throng inside the large room and her plan altered. She'd slip away in a few minutes, while everyone was otherwise occupied. They'd assume she'd just met up with some other people in this crowd and wouldn't give it a second thought.

Someone put a glass in her hand. Tin Man took Koala off to dance to make up for his gaffe and Humpty and Sister Sam found a group of colleagues and were busy comparing outfits and guessing identities.

Philly stood on the fringe of the group, planning her escape. Just her luck to run into Sam! At least he hadn't recognised her. Father Time stood, scythe in hand, just across from her, a large fob watch conveniently around his neck. Already after nine.

She'd give it just a few minutes and then she'd steal away and go home.

She was a goddess!

He was wending his way through the crowded room, enjoying the anonymity lent by his disguise, dropping in to catch snatches of conversation with this group and that, when he saw her. Even in this sea of costumes and colour she stood out like a beacon. How could she not, looking like an Egyptian queen?

She wasn't tall yet her legs had to be sensational under the sleek gown that looked as sheer and fine as gossamer, accentuating the feminine curves apparent beneath. Golden sandals peeped out below.

The gown ended at her breasts with some sort of twist of the fabric in a strapless arrangement that hugged her form and had him immediately calculating how difficult it would be to get off. Her lips were a splash of red, vibrant and lush and a contrast against the jet-black hair swishing over her bare shoulders. Coiled bracelets adorned her arms.

Her costume was unmistakeable. She was Cleopatra, Queen of the Nile. Little wonder emperors had fallen under her spell.

He drank in every detail and his prolonged scrutiny confirmed what he'd known immediately.

He wanted her.

Who was she? With her mask covering her eyes there was no way he could pin down her identity. Did she work for him or was she someone's partner?

He scoured the group she was standing in, but no one guarded her possessively, no one fielded admirers. She had to be alone. No one in their right mind would let her fly solo in such an outfit. If she was his date he wouldn't let her out of his sight.

Who was he trying to kid? If she was his date he wouldn't let her out of his bed.

He had to have her.

Two minutes. Just two minutes more and she'd excuse herself. They wouldn't miss her now. Sister Sam and Humpty were both deep in conversation with Noddy and Big Ears. She'd leave, make the excuse of a headache if anyone asked her, but chances were no one would even notice in this crowd.

Escape was at hand.

She placed her barely touched glass of champagne on the tray of a passing waiter and slid into the crowd, heading for the door. The sudden hand around her arm told her she hadn't made the clean escape she was hoping for.

'You're not leaving?'

She stopped dead as the tremor passed through her, but there was no mistake.

It was him!

She'd know Damien DeLuca's autocratic voice anywhere. But now his tone held something else— interest?—*desire?* She turned and gasped. Relieved her mask would hide the shock in her eyes—the admiration in her eyes—she drank him in. He looked sensational, from the overlapping metal plates at his shoulders to the carved breastplate and the slatted leather tunic ending above his knees. His arms were bare, olive-skinned and gleaming, except for some sort of wide band at his wrist. He held a helmet under one arm, a sword hung at his side.

A Roman gladiator or an emperor going off to lead his army to war? Whatever, he looked magnificent. He fitted the part, with his Italian colouring, hair lazily windswept, curling at his collar and with his chiselled cheekbones accentuated by the simple mask tied over his eyes.

If she'd thought he'd exuded masculine sex appeal in a suit, that was nothing to the sheer testosterone surge he gave off in this outfit.

She swallowed and looked back towards the door. His hand still held her arm and the heat from his grip weakened her resolve to leave.

'Stay, Cleopatra,' he said intently, almost reverently. 'I've been waiting over two thousand years to find you again.'

She shuddered, his words going straight through her in a flush of heat that seemed to touch and awaken every last extremity of her and then bounce back, settling at her core, warm and heavy. He reached across and took her hand.

'Surely you recognise me? Mark Antony?'

He inclined his head and for the first time she allowed herself to smile. It was Damien—*really Damien*—and he'd noticed her, amongst all these people. And not only had he noticed her; if she wasn't mistaken he was coming on to her.

Her head dipped in response; she couldn't allow herself to speak. Her brain had too much information to process to cope with making small conversation. Besides, why spoil this magic? He thought he'd found Cleopatra. Why let on just yet that she was Philly from marketing? He wouldn't hang around two minutes if he knew. Tonight she might just stick to being Cleopatra.

'Come,' he said, tugging on her hand so that she came closer to his body, closer to the source of that heat, as he gestured to the dimly lit dance floor beyond. 'Dance with me.'

She didn't have to think about whether or not she should; her feet drifted after him of their own accord, her plan to exit all but forgotten. He led her to the dance floor and drew her into his arms, his hand at her back anchoring her close, his other hand wrapped around hers, securing it close to his shoulder, his wide shoulder, the armour enhancing his masculine form.

'You're beautiful,' he said, his voice low and husky.

His words tripped her heartbeat. *Beautiful.* No one had told her that for a very long time. She had to remember to breathe and when she did it was with a gasp that immediately rewarded her with the scent of him—masculine, clean and enriched with the smell of leather. But not just his scent. She was sure she could just about taste him.

He started swaying to the song, taking her with him, their bodies moving in unison as the music took them away.

Heaven. This must be what heaven was like. Sheer bliss. She closed her eyes, allowing herself to be carried along by the music and by the man who held her in his arms with such strength, yet such tenderness.

Suddenly he stopped. She blinked her eyes open, the music still playing, and saw Damien's head swivelled to the side. He was talking to someone; it looked like a geisha but the voice was unmistakably Enid's. She caught a snatch of her words here and there— *London—crisis*—and Damien rattled off something in response and the geisha disappeared.

He turned his face back to hers, the line of his mouth grim, tension replacing the liquid heat she'd felt within his grasp.

'I have to take a phone call.'

His arms continued to surround her and he stared at her as if he was wavering between the phone call and the woman in his arms. 'I'll be back. Ten minutes max.' He hesitated. 'Maybe twenty.'

She looked up at him, his face so close to her own,

and she knew she would wait forever if it meant feeling like this again. Then he dipped his head and his lips brushed hers, so gently that his breath was as much a part of the kiss, as much a part of the sensation, as his lips.

'So beautiful,' he whispered, his voice suddenly rougher. 'Wait for me.' He smiled and let her go.

And then he was gone.

It was like being in a vacuum. Damien had gone, all too quickly, and she felt cold, suddenly bereft of his heat. *But he'd be back.* He'd promised he'd be back. And that knowledge started the warmth pooling inside her all over again.

For a moment longer she stood, all by herself, in the centre of the crowded dance floor, couples jostling for space all around until she realised she had to move.

Ten minutes, he'd said. Maybe twenty. Where should she wait for him? How would he find her?

She made her way to the bar, ordered a mineral water and held the iced glass to her cheeks, trying to think about the time, trying not to think about the time. How many minutes now—five?—ten? She wanted to be back in his arms and every minute he was away felt like for ever.

The band finished its set and the dancers dispersed as someone took over the microphone. A stand-up comic. Good. At least that might take her mind off the time.

Damien cursed, loud and emphatic, before turning the microphone on the speaker telephone back up. It was worse than he'd thought. Enid sat nearby, armed with pen and paper and tactfully ignoring his comments, her delicately made-up white face giving nothing away.

He raked a hand through his hair, waiting for someone to pick up, snagging it on the mask. He tore it off, flinging it down on the desk of the makeshift office. It was actually a storeroom but with her usual efficient style Enid had already organised a couple of chairs, a phone and a fax machine. He didn't need a computer—this was no time for email. He wanted action.

Of all the times for Delucatek's United Kingdom agent to collapse. The news had been splashed in London's Saturday papers and now there were a hundred clients all screaming for help. Okay, these things happened in business. He'd dealt with worse before and no doubt there'd be worse to come, but why did it have to be tonight? Why now? Already he'd been here forty minutes but he wasn't going anywhere until he'd cornered his agent's CEO. There were plenty of questions he wanted to ask him.

He picked up a pencil, tapping it furiously on the table as he waited.

Strains of laughter drifted in from the nearby auditorium and his mind wandered back to the ball and the woman he'd left behind. She was waiting for him. Or at least he hoped she was.

He could still feel her in his arms, the magic way her body floated into his, matching his moves and the music so that her sweet body flowed, her curves swaying to the rhythm. How he'd like to feel that body sway to a different rhythm, how he'd like to feel her body dance to a different music, a music they would make together. His body ached just thinking about it. He was a normal man; he liked sex. But it had been a long time since he'd wanted anyone as much as he wanted her.

There was something about her. Something special. That body, those lush lips. The way she'd come as Cleopatra, Mark Antony's seductress. That had to be fate.

He glanced again at his watch. What if she'd found someone else? The thought of her with another man— holding her, dancing with her, maybe even... His teeth ground together. She'd tasted so sweet, so ripe. The mere idea that someone else was sampling her mouth or even something more...

The pencil in his hand snapped in two.

At the other end of the line the phone rang out. Damien slammed down the receiver and checked his notes for the next number. He'd track this guy down and get him to take responsibility for this mess if it killed him.

He wasn't coming back. The sad truth hit her like a blow to the gut. Almost two hours now. The comedian had finished, the band had done another two brackets, leaving taped music in its wake, and it was clear there was no way Damien was coming back. Either whatever had called him away was taking more time than he'd anticipated or he'd found someone else and changed his mind.

There was no question as to which scenario was the most likely. She'd been kidding herself to think she was that special.

It was getting late. She should go home. Staying here longer just increased the feeling of bitterness, the sense of overwhelming loss that gradually but irrevocably gnawed away at her earlier euphoria.

He wasn't coming back.

She had one last look around the ballroom. The party was in full swing and laughter and music filled the air. Her evening hadn't been a total loss. She'd chatted with a few people, sticking to safe topics like costumes and the party. She'd enjoyed the comedian. Even the lavishly spread tables, covered with all manner of finger food and nibbles, had proved a diversion, at least for her eyes, helping for a little while to take her mind off the time and its passing.

But now it was time to go home. There was no point staying. She put her glass down and turned towards the exit.

'Would you care to dance with me?'

She smiled her thanks at the six foot tall kangaroo looking down at her and shook her head. 'I was just leaving but thank you.'

'Just one dance before you go? Come on, it'll be fun. You ever danced with a kangaroo before?'

'Um, no actually.'

'Then now's your chance.' The kangaroo held out its paw.

She laughed a little and slipped her arm through his furry one. 'Well, if you put it like that.' One dance wouldn't hurt. It would be nothing like dancing with Damien had been, but it might be fun, and it would be something to tell her mother in the morning. She'd certainly enjoy a story like this.

Kanga made it to the dance floor in a combination of skips and hops that had Philly laughing before they'd even begun. When he started to move to the music she couldn't stop. She was either being buffeted by the huge hind legs of his costume or he'd swing around and collect her with his tail. It was impossible not to have fun.

She was still here.

For a while he'd been unable to find her, scared beyond belief that she'd already left when he didn't even know who she was. But then his eyes had been drawn to the dance floor and there she was.

My God, she was even more beautiful than he remembered. Her smile was so wide her whole face lit up and she moved so well to the fast rock and roll number, her body picking up the beat and making it her own.

He checked out her partner and discounted him in the same glance. He could deal with Skippy. He'd dealt with much stronger adversaries, like the CEO he'd finally caught up with. He was history in the business community from here on in.

He moved closer, sensing the music track was nearing its end, preparing to cut in before anyone else had a chance to get anywhere near her. He'd wasted enough time tonight. Now he was going to make her his.

What made her look around? There was no way she could have heard a thing over the loud music, but something made her turn. Something made her look.

Not something.

Someone.

Her steps faltered in time with the skip of her heartbeat.

Damien. He was back and he was heading straight towards her. He'd come back for her. She sucked in a breath, watching his approach. He looked like a triumphant general returning from war. She was unaware she'd stopped dancing until Kanga tapped her on the shoulder with his paw.

'You tired? It's like an oven inside here. I'm getting a drink. Want one?'

She was aware her head was shaking but only just. Every other part of her concentrated on Damien's purposeful approach, her body tingling in mounting anticipation with each step he took closer. His eyes were still masked but she could tell his focus didn't leave her. It was empowering knowing that he could no more take his eyes off her than she could from him.

'Okay, then. Thanks for the dance.' Kanga bounded off to find refreshments as Damien reached her side. He took one of her hands, lifted it to his mouth and held it there, pressed to his lips.

Finally he removed his mouth. 'Now,' he said, 'where were we?'

His grip was firm, his hand warm and strong. The fast rock and roll number came to an end as, without letting go of her hand, he drew her closer. For a few seconds he just stood, looking at her, ignoring the jostling of the crowd around him, waiting for the new track to cut in.

She couldn't move. Even if he hadn't had a grip on her hand, she wasn't going anywhere. From under his mask the heat from his gaze pulled her like a magnet. Her body responded, breasts swelling, nipples tightening, as his sheer presence touched her in places his eyes couldn't.

When the gentle strains of guitar playing signalled the start of a slow Robbie Williams ballad Damien pulled her gently into his arms and suddenly he was all around her. His chest, solid and warm, pressing against hers, his thighs firm, his arms encasing her, modelling her like clay to his form while he swayed to the music.

She gave in to the pressure and let her head fall against his chest to rest upon the plates that covered it. It wasn't exactly comfortable but she didn't care. When she breathed in it was his scent, natural and masculine, that intoxicated her senses.

His large hands held her close, one cradling her shoulder, the other firm at the small of her back, and his head rested over hers as they moved together to the music, their bodies as close as they could be with clothes on.

He breathed deep, unable to get a hold on her scent—frustrating for someone who prided himself on knowing them backwards. She was wearing a wig—that didn't help—but there was some kind of rich perfume, something exotic, just like she was. Something else lurked below too, but the signals were blurry and he couldn't quite make it out. Whatever it was, she smelt all woman. He liked that.

The rest of her he could make out just fine. She fitted him perfectly. Something told him she'd fit him *everywhere* perfectly. She moulded to his body as if she was made for it. The jut of her breasts, soft but firm against his chest, the dip to her waist and the flare of her hips. She was perfect.

His hands moved slowly over her back, exploring, taking inventory. He liked what he felt as she followed his swaying rhythm, her body curvy and sensual and just the way he liked them.

The only thing he hated was the mask she wore. He'd do away with that the first chance he got.

Besides, he wanted to see her eyes when she came.

He stiffened at the thought and the reality of his situation hit him like a brick. He wasn't sure how the Romans had coped, but the thought of his costume betraying his desire on the dance floor in front of five hundred employees and their partners wasn't appealing. He had to get them both out of here, now, while he could still think straight.

The music track had reached its climax. He was vaguely envious as it wound down to a slow refrain. There was no way he was winding down any time soon—unless this woman had something to do with it. And if he had any say she'd have everything to do with it!

'Let's get out of here,' he whispered, nibbling on her ear.

She felt too weak to respond, lost in the multitude of new and wonderful sensations she was being bombarded with.

Was this how seduction felt? Never before had she felt such liquid heat pooling inside her. This total absence of real thought, all mind function replaced by body function and totally concentrated on one thing, the fruition of one act. One utterly irresistible, inevitable act.

She wanted more of what he was doing to her, more of what he was making her feel. She wanted him.

This was new—to feel such intense longing and desire for any one man! Passion like she'd never before experienced. Bryce had never once made her feel like this in their entire two-year relationship. He'd always made her feel that lovemaking was an obligation.

What was happening now with Damien couldn't be

more different. Right now making love with Damien felt like her destiny. A destiny she felt powerless to deny.

With his hand at her back steering her towards an exit, she allowed him to propel her towards that destiny.

He swooped and opened a side door in her path, his other hand encouraging her through to the dimly lit hallway beyond. He pulled the door shut behind them and spun her against the wall in the same rapid-fire action.

Her back met the wall at the same instant his mouth meshed with hers.

Frantic.

Hungry.

His lips slanted over hers and a moment later he was inside, his tongue seeking hers. He tasted rich and real, of masculine heat and warm brandy, and she let herself go with the sensation, the ecstasy of him filling her mouth.

One hand found her breast and she gasped as his fingers grazed her nipple, searing through the light fabric.

The other dropped to her skirt and he filled his hand with the round of one perfect cheek. Her muscles tightened in response and he was rewarded by the push of her belly into his growing hardness.

He growled, long and low, at the building tension, the anticipation of its relief, and she squirmed under his hands.

His touch was a brand on her, exploring, pushing, urgent and hot. Need radiated inside her like a fire front, the flames spreading wider until every part of her was alight. The oxygen delivered by her rapid breaths fuelled the flames.

The door alongside swung open. Someone looked around, mumbling a quick apology before diving back into the auditorium. Damien pulled his mouth away giving a low soft curse. He grabbed her hand again. 'Come on,' he said.

She followed behind him down the corridor, senses reeling as he tugged her insistently along, then round a corner, up a flight of stairs and over a parquet floor. He stopped outside a pair of solid doors flanked with impressive brass framing. The boardroom. He pulled something from a pocket somewhere—a keycard—and shoved it through the slot. In the wooden surrounds and over the muted sounds of the revelry below the click echoed loud and long. *And final.*

She swallowed as logic fought for precedence in her mind. Once inside there was no turning back. No chance to change her mind.

But she had no intention of changing her mind. There was no way she didn't want to follow this scene through to its logical conclusion. She'd come too far.

He pulled her into the room, though she hardly needed persuading. The door closed behind them and he turned the lock. They were alone, the room unlit but for the venetian blind dressed window sending slices of moonlight cascading across the sleek boardroom table.

Her eyes adjusted and in the gloom it was as if the years had peeled away and history itself was replaying.

Right now she was Cleopatra and he was her Mark Antony.

He reached out a hand to her face, touching her mask.

She flinched from his grasp and shook her head. 'No!' she whispered. She wouldn't kid herself. He wouldn't be doing this if he knew who she was. Only after, when it was too late for him to change his mind, only then would she let him take off her mask.

He would be angry, no doubt. Even worse, he would be disappointed. His fantasy would end right then and there. But she would have this memory to treasure for ever. And, no doubt, she would.

In the pale moonlight she saw the corner of his mouth lift. 'All right, let's do it your way. I have more urgent business first.'

His hands went to her waist and he lifted her easily to the table, pushing away the chairs to each side. He eased down the bodice of her gown, releasing her breasts to the air and his gaze. Her skin tightened, her nipples achingly firm.

He growled low and rough, and dropped his mouth to one pert peak. Her swift intake of breath pushed her breast further towards him; he filled his mouth with the flesh as his tongue traced the tip. He left that breast, focused on the second, delivering the same languid pleasure strokes with his tongue, his hands now at her legs, running her gown up her bare legs, spreading them as he forced himself between.

She clung to his head, her fingers raking through his hair, down his neck, exploring his wide shoulders, drinking in the width and strength of his back.

One hand rounded her thigh and against the fabric of her thong. The damp fabric of her thong. 'Oh, God,' he muttered as her head fell back, his fingers continuing their gentle exploration, the fabric no barrier to flesh already inflamed and exquisitely sensitised. She clawed at his costume, attempting to fill her own hands with the touch of his skin, frustrated that she could find no way in.

Suddenly he wheeled away, impatiently pulling at his garments, shucking off the shoulder gear and chest plate with a clatter and tearing off his tunic. He returned to her, naked but for his black underwear and his sandals, his skin gleaming in the soft moonlight.

She pulled him into her arms and relished the feel of the skin at his back, hot and slick with expectation and desire, as he continued his exploration, driving her crazy with need as he teased her with his fingers.

'So beautiful,' he murmured against her nipple. 'And so wet.' Those last words sounded as if they had been wrung from him. He lifted her slightly and removed her thong and with both hands he pulled her closer to the edge of the table. His underwear was no barrier to the hard bulge of his erection butting against her.

He was so big.

Anticipation kicked up a notch. She wanted him inside her. All of him. He pulled himself away fractionally, wrenching down his own underwear. And then he was free. Even in the dim light he looked magnificent, all pulsing energy with its own special rhythm. She reached down a hand, wanting to feel the power, to guide him to her, to share the dance.

She touched him, her fingers cupping him, entranced by the weight, the contrasts in the feel of him, rock-hard yet with skin like silk, so rigid yet pulsing, filled with life.

She closed her fingers around him and he gasped. This fantasy woman would not escape him tonight.

He had to have her. Had to feel her wrapped around him, hugging him tight inside, her muscles clamping around him in spasms when she came.

Her hand moved the length of him, her thumb flicking over his sensitive tip.

Oh, God!

Exit rational thought.

He grabbed her wrist, pulling her hand away as he scooped her yet closer, directing himself at the same time that he dropped his mouth on hers. His rapid action took her by surprise—her lips already open and forming a surprised 'o' even as he plundered her mouth with his. And then he brought her closer still, until her legs wrapped around behind him and her slick wetness welcomed him, urging him to drive himself home.

He didn't need further invitation. With one smooth thrust he entered her, wrapping himself in liquid velvet. She cried out something indiscernible, but even muffled by his mouth over hers he recognised the same note of victory and ecstasy he'd felt in joining her.

She felt magnificent.

Slowly he withdrew, only to slam into her again, leaning into her and forcing her lower. Her hands went back to support herself and she threw her head back, gasping for air, her shiny fake hair falling back from her pale skin like the tide receding.

He loved the way it moved.

He loved the way she moved, especially when he was inside her.

He planted his mouth over her throat in the spot where her pulse flickered and jumped as he pumped into her again. She felt so good, so damned good, and as she squeezed her muscles around him and the pressure built inside he knew that though he wanted this feeling to last longer, for ever, there was no way he was going to be able to make it last.

No way on earth.

There was nothing he could do. Control ceased to exist. Then she bucked under him, her muscles tight and urgent, inflaming, drawing him deeper and deeper inside and he was lost.

He cried out, something harsh and guttural and triumphant as he emptied himself into her shuddering body, collecting her up and pulling her down on to him in a broad conference chair.

Oh, wow!

She hadn't known what to expect but it sure hadn't been such an all-consuming experience. Her body still hummed from their union, her pulse and breathing slowly settling back into a more normal routine.

He sprawled below her, cradling her, as her brain tried to kick back in.

But what had she done?

She took a few deep breaths, feeling her pulse quieten and trying to make sense of what had just happened.

She'd just made love with the boss. And not just any boss. She'd made love with Damien DeLuca.

What was more, they'd not used protection. Nothing. Hadn't even stopped to think about it.

She must be mad. She'd thought she wasn't the reckless type but one feeling of desire, one whiff of Damien being attracted to her, and logic had vanished from her mind. Completely and utterly.

She must be crazy.

And now she was cradled on top of him, Damien's

hand at her breast, caressing her, his naked body be-low already showing signs of recovery.

The languid feel of her muscles and limbs vanished as cold, hard truth replaced it. Without trying to touch him too much, she tried to angle herself off, tried to edge away. How was she going to explain what had happened? How could she ever face him again? Guilt and shame settled upon her like a shroud.

She had to get out of here. Before he discovered who she was. There was even a chance she might even lose her job over this—who knew how he might react?—and she couldn't afford that, not with the prospect of expensive hospice care for her mother coming up some time soon.

She had to get out of here. *Now*.

'What's wrong?'

She glanced at the door and her pulse went into overdrive as an idea formed in her mind. With Damien naked, at least she had a running start. Her hand patted her throat. 'Th…thirsty.'

'I think I can fix that,' he said easily, easing her from his lap gently.

She pulled up the bodice on her dress and reached down to retrieve her underwear.

'Don't bother putting that back on,' he said, leaning over to kiss her on her already swollen lips. 'We haven't finished with each other yet. Not by a long shot.'

Still she clung to the scrap of material as if it was life-support while his words turned to a desire that curled deep within her.

He wanted her again.

She wished he hadn't told her that. She didn't want any regrets from this night—she had enough of those already. But the last thing she wanted was to lie by herself in bed during the long lonely nights ahead thinking about what pleasures she might have missed out on.

Naked, he turned and padded his way to a built-in cabinet along the narrowest wall. She watched him go in the pale light even as she edged closer to the door, his skin deliciously firm, his legs long and powerful, unwilling to tear her eyes away. He pulled open a door, exposing a bar fridge behind and hunkered down to look inside.

This was her chance!

She hit the door running, doing battle with the lock and finally wrenching it open. Behind her he shouted for her to stop but she couldn't stop, couldn't turn.

She raced over the parquet floor to the stairs as fast as she could, the heels on her sandals clattering and echoing in the dark-filled space, blood pumping so loudly it drowned out the curses ringing in her ears.

She was down the steps and halfway to the exit before she calmed to a brisk walk, heading purposefully for the safety of the night, ears straining over the music for anything that would signal less than a clean getaway. But behind her came no sound of pursuit, no hint of a chase.

She was going to make it. Euphoria replaced panic. She was safe.

CHAPTER FOUR

SHE was a mess of nerves.

On Monday morning Philly sat at her desk, responding to emails and organising herself for the day and the week ahead. Walking into the office had been hairy—everyone had been talking about the ball, laughing about the costumes and the night's revelries.

She'd purposely avoided talk of the ball, hinting at a quiet night at home with her mother—and had waited with breath frozen in her lungs for someone to out her. If anyone had recognised her, this was it. But her colleagues just expressed their sympathies that she'd missed the event of the year and drifted away to talk amongst themselves. Even Sam just grunted and headed off for a meeting with Damien.

Thank heavens Sam had recovered from the flu— she didn't fancy running into Damien DeLuca right now. She wasn't at all sure how she would ever face him again.

At least now Sam was back from sick leave and holding the reins again and she could keep a low profile. Sam would certainly make sure of it.

She was mid-sentence in a response to a lengthy email when the phone rang. She propped the phone up to her ear, still typing, with her train of thought still focused on her detailed reply.

'Ms Summers?' Damien's voice belted down the line faster than she could make her own greeting. Her body tensed on a shiver and the phone dropped from her shoulder, landing on the desk with a loud thunk. The noise snapped her out of her temporary paralysis and she grappled for the receiver. Why was Damien calling her?

Did he know? Had Sam recognised her after all and informed Damien of her identity?

'What the— Ms Summers, is that you?'

'S-sorry,' she stammered. 'The phone slipped.'

She heard something like an exasperated sigh and could imagine the rolling of eyes going on at the other end of the line.

'Ms Summers, I need you in my office. Now.'

Philly clutched the phone. She wasn't ready for this. How was she going to explain what had happened? How could she look him in the eye after what they'd done together, the intimacy they'd shared?

She was bound to get the sack over this. She didn't deserve anything less. How was she going to explain that to her next prospective employer?

'Are you still there?'

She swallowed. 'I'll be right up,' she croaked.

He slapped the phone down, regarding it critically. What was her problem? He hoped he wasn't making a big mistake over this.

He turned back to Sam, who was waiting anxiously in the chair opposite, scraping at his fingertips with his thumbnail and looking every inch a man insecure about his position in the world.

Right now Damien knew the feeling. He'd had it ever since the woman dressed as Cleopatra had abandoned him on Saturday night. No one had ever walked out on Damien DeLuca before—that was bad enough. But right now there was a woman out there who'd done even more than that—she'd run out on him and he didn't even have a clue who she was.

It had only taken him a few seconds to throw his costume back on but by the time he'd done that and raced downstairs there'd been no sign of her anywhere. She'd been swallowed up by the night.

What was her game?

Why had she run away like that? Why had she panicked? She'd had plenty of opportunity to change her mind if she'd so wanted—and she hadn't wanted—that much was patently clear. On the contrary, she'd been perfectly willing all the way—perfectly accommodating—perfectly inviting.

A perfect fit.

He'd been cheated of exploring that knowledge further. He'd been cheated of seeing how far they could take each other. He'd been cheated of seeing her eyes...

Could it be that she'd recognised him? Was that what had scared her off? Suddenly afraid of being with the company founder and CEO she'd fled? But she hadn't seemed that obtuse—surely she would have realised when he'd been called away suddenly by Enid, if not before, of his true identity? So why would she suddenly panic later on?

He didn't like it one bit—the prospect of her knowing his identity when he had no idea who she was or where to start looking for her. He studied the man sitting nervously opposite him.

But Sam might.

When the masks had come off he was sure he'd seen Sam dressed up as a nun. There'd been a nun in the group where he'd first seen the woman standing. He might know. And if Sam didn't someone else had to. She'd been there for hours waiting for him to return. Someone had to have spoken to her, someone had to know who she was.

'Sam,' he said, adding a smile for good measure. 'Did you have a good time on Saturday night?'

Sam chortled and sat up, eager to please. 'A great time. Wonderful party. Just wonderful. The staff are very grateful to you—'

Damien held up one hand. 'Good, that's fine. But I wonder if you can help me with something.'

'Anything—name it.'

'Only there's someone there I meant to catch up with before the end but I missed her. She was dressed up as Cleopatra. Dark hair, white gown—sound familiar at all?'

'Too right, she does,' said Sam enthusiastically before he suddenly frowned. 'Not sure where she got to, actually—one moment she was there and the next—poof—she was gone.'

Damien felt his pulse kick up. He was on the trail. Hot on the trail. She wouldn't stay out of his clutches for long. 'And her name,' he prompted. 'Can you tell me her name?'

Sam thought for a moment. 'She did tell me.' He looked ceilingwards and scratched his chin while Damien resisted the urge to slam his fist into it. If he thought it would jog his memory the fist would have won hands down.

'Oh, that's it. I remember now.' Sam looked triumphant. Damien tried to remain seated.

'And?'

'Marie, from the Sydney office I think she said. Didn't catch a surname. She was a little bit wary of going in—must have been off-putting, not knowing anybody at one of those things. Awkward when you hardly know a soul. She came in with us but then we lost contact with her.' He frowned, contemplating his nails. 'Wonder where she got to?'

Damien knew something of where she'd disappeared to. He'd asked her to dance and at first she'd seemed reluctant but then something had changed and she'd moved like warm chocolate in his arms—soft, luscious and ready to be consumed.

Very ready as it later turned out when he'd returned from his calls. She'd waited for him for way longer than what he'd promised. But she'd waited for him as if she could no sooner forsake the hope he'd return than he could abandon the absolute necessity to get back to her.

Then she'd fallen into his arms and the tension had built between them again. The trek to the boardroom had been an exercise in restraint but he'd made it and she was every bit a willing partner when they'd got there. More than willing, he recalled, as she'd practically invited him to enter her. And he had.

It had been like a dream. The sex had been everything he'd anticipated with the promise of more, even more mind-blowing. And then she'd gone and his evening had turned into a nightmare.

Sam continued to prattle on, openly contemplating where Marie might have gone. Damien ignored him, diving instead for his internal phone directory, scouring the lists. The Sydney office wasn't large and the name didn't ring any bells but the way this company was growing there was no way he could keep up with all the new staff.

He made one unsuccessful pass through. No luck.

Too fast, he decided, and set his eyes to something less than warp speed as he scanned the lists.

No Marie!

He picked up the phone, oblivious to the stream of consciousness coming from Sam's direction. 'Enid,' he snapped as soon as she answered, 'have we taken on anyone recently in the Sydney office called Marie? There's no one on the phone lists.'

He waited the few seconds while Enid responded in the negative before then throwing the phone down in disgust.

'Are you sure it was Marie?'

'What? Oh, er…' Sam thought for a moment before nodding his head. 'Pretty sure. I tend to take more notice of what people say when they're such stunners, if you get my drift.'

Damien sent him a look that would curdle milk and watched Sam shrink down in his chair with some satisfaction. He wasn't entirely comfortable with the thought that every other man in the room had felt the same powerful attraction to his mystery woman. 'No, I'm not sure I do.'

But what Sam had said bothered him. His mystery woman had chosen a fake name to go with her fake outfit. Now how was he going to find her?

It had to be someone who worked in the company. One of maybe three hundred women. Half of them he could write off as being too old, a good percentage of those left didn't have the same kind of head turning figure. There couldn't be more than one hundred who'd qualify. He'd find her, whatever it took. And when he found her…

A tap at the door shifted his attention from Sam.

'You wanted to see me?'

Miss Brown Mouse stood at the door, looking even more timid than her creature companion as her eyes scampered around the room, settling finally somewhere near Sam.

'Ms Summers,' Damien said, turning his mind back to business. 'I've been waiting for you. Come in.'

She took tentative mouse steps across the room, finally lowering herself into a vacant chair alongside Sam. She was wearing the same brown jacket as the first time he'd met her, but this time with matching trousers. They fitted her better than the skirt; at least they gave some sense that she had legs, decent ones by the look, under all that tweed.

For just a second his gaze narrowed, his thoughts scrambling for sense. Surely she couldn't be one of the one hundred most likely? He looked to her face, pink and shy, her lips tight and her eyes skittering from side to side.

No, no chance. But she might know who his Cleopatra was. 'Were you at the ball on the weekend?'

She jumped as if she'd been shot but it was Sam who responded. 'Philly wasn't there.'

Damien looked from Sam to Philly. 'Why was that?'

'Well, you see,' she said, licking her lips, not wanting to add lying to her list of transgressions, 'my mother isn't well…'

He seemed to think about it for a while and then he nodded.

Philly couldn't wait to get out of there. She wasn't sure what had just happened here, but it looked as if she'd managed to survive, her secret identity intact.

'So,' she said. 'If that's all?' Her hands were already pushing her up out of the chair.

'No, that's not all. Sit down.'

She obeyed him, not because she wanted to, but more to do with the fact that her knees had turned to jelly, the exhilaration at her near escape evaporating.

'I asked you in here because I need someone to work closely on a new project with me. After that presentation you delivered the other week, I figure you're just the person for the job so I asked Sam if he could do without you for a few days.'

She looked desperately at the man next to her. Surely he wouldn't let anyone else get an opportunity this good? 'And Sam said?'

'Sam said he couldn't spare you.'

She let go of a breath she'd been holding. Good old gatekeeper Sam—never let someone else get an opportunity you might want yourself. Maybe he wasn't such a bad supervisor after all.

'But I told him he had no choice.'

His words were like a punch to her lungs and she scrambled for air in the wake of his announcement.

'So it's all settled.' He turned to Sam and gave him a brief nod and a look that had him dismissed and heading for the door before Damien turned his focus back on her. 'Enid will arrange to have your work station things moved up here—there's a spare office just down the hall. We've got three days before we have to be in Queensland for meetings at the Gold Coast. We have to move fast on this. It's an opportunity too good to miss. Palmcorp is a rapidly growing business whose needs have outstripped their current systems. If we get on the ground floor with this company, it will be worth millions to us.'

'The Gold Coast,' she muttered. *With Damien.* She gulped. No, that was the last thing she needed. 'But I can't...'

He looked up sharply. 'Can't what?'

'I can't go with you.'

'What do you mean?'

I don't want to go with you!

'Well, for one thing I can't just up and leave my mother. I told you. She's ill.'

'So who looks after her now, while you're at work?'

'No one.' She noticed the victorious look in his eyes, as if he'd just scored a winning goal in the dying minutes of the Aussie Rules football grand final, and she longed to vanquish it, longed to have the umpire declare it a no goal. 'But I don't like to leave her alone at night, just the same.'

'I don't want anyone else for this presentation. I want you.'

'Well, you're just going to have to find someone else. I can't go. I won't go.'

'I see.'

The grinding of his teeth told her he didn't see at all.

'And what's the other reason?'

She looked up, confused. 'Other reason?'

'You said before, *for one thing* you had to look after your mother. What's the other reason you don't want to come to Brisbane with me?'

'Oh.' She shrugged as she felt the colour and heat flood back to her face. 'It's just a... a figure of speech.'

His piercing eyes continued to assess her, as if weighing up her words, stripping right through the layers of her deceit. But he couldn't see that far. He didn't know. He couldn't know.

She shrugged. 'What other reason could there be?'

'Are you worried I might seduce you? Is that what this is about?'

Her lungs sucked in air like a drowning woman coming up for oxygen.

'Because, let me assure you, there is no chance of that. *Absolutely no chance.* This is a business deal. I need your professional help, so if that's what's worrying you, forget it. Right now.'

Philly battled to regain her mental balance. There he was trying to put her mind at rest. If only he knew! She could ignore the implication that she wasn't worth seducing if she didn't have to explain her real reasons for not wanting to go with him.

'Of course. That's what I'd expect.'

'Good. Now that we've established that, once I arrange for round-the-clock nursing for your mother, I take it you'll have no objections to accompanying me?'

His words were framed as a question but the tone he used made them more like a challenge. She opened her mouth to talk but nothing came out.

'Fine,' he said. 'That looks like it's settled then.'

He picked up the phone and started issuing instructions to Enid regarding moving Philly's office upstairs, arranging their flight bookings and organising a round-the-clock nursing service. She sat there, looking across at him, her blood heating at his complete disrespect of her wishes, not to mention her desires.

She still hadn't agreed to go with him. How was her mother going to react to having a stranger in the house, even if there was the bonus that she'd have someone to look after her twenty-four hours a day? He hadn't even given Philly the chance to ask her.

'How dare you?' she said, rising to her feet as finally he returned the phone to the cradle. 'How dare you make arrangements for my family to suit yourself? How would you like it if I went around organising your family, so you could fall in with whatever my plans were?'

He looked up at her, his eyes for once strangely empty.

'If that pleases you, go right ahead. But you might have some trouble. My whole family was wiped out when I was nine years old.'

CHAPTER FIVE

THE words hung between them like lead weights in the still air of the climate-controlled office, the hum of his laptop the only sound.

'I'm sorry,' she said, standing there awkwardly, unsure whether to stay or leave.

'Don't be,' he said without looking up. 'It wasn't your fault.'

'No, I mean…' Her hands found each other, together they wrestled for the right words. 'I mean—'

'Forget it,' he said with a sweep of his hand, as if it meant nothing to him. 'We've got a lot to get through today so I suggest you get yourself organised. I want you back here in half an hour so we can get started.'

Fine, she thought, *whatever you say*, her compassion evaporating at his dry tone. She nodded though she was sure he didn't notice; his head was already focused on the papers in front of him. She turned to leave.

'Oh, and Ms Summers—'

'Yes?'

'Do you have anything to wear that's not brown?'

Philly looked down at her jacket and trousers. Okay, so what was wrong with her clothes? Maybe the suit didn't have an expensive label, but it was a good name brand and it had been an absolute bargain, even if the jacket was a size too large.

'You have a problem with brown?' She could, of course, tell him she had a little Egyptian number stashed away at home waiting to be returned that was a real crowd pleaser, but somehow she didn't think that was what he had in mind.

'This deal's worth a lot to Delucatek. The people we'll be dealing with are real high-flyers. We should look the part. Do you have anything suitable?'

Meaning *she* should look the part. His suit smacked of designer while hers screamed bargain basement. She mentally flicked through her wardrobe's contents, more spartan than ever after a pre-wedding economy drive. Bryce had been keen to get a property portfolio established between them as soon as possible and she'd been on a strict budget. Of course, she hadn't realised that at the same time that she was budgeting, he was out splashing everything he could on the other woman, Miss Hot-Property.

All her scrimping hadn't left much in the way of spending money though, especially for new clothes. Three suits, one tan, one summer-weight beige and the tweed she had on, plus black trousers, assorted blouses and a winter jacket was all that quickly came to mind if she didn't count one pristine wedding dress still in its cellophane wrapping. She really ought to think about returning that some time. She wouldn't be using it now.

She could have used her savings to buy new clothes since then, of course. But there was every possibility she'd need all of that and more once her mother got too sick to stay at home.

She was no fool. As much as she wanted to be able to care for her mother, there would come a time when it just wouldn't work. She wouldn't be able to be there twenty-four hours a day and she'd need to move somewhere with better care options. And from the enquiries she'd already made, good hospice care didn't come cheap.

'I don't know,' she said honestly. 'What will I need?'

He barely looked up. 'See Enid later. She'll have the schedule and you can work out what you have to get and go shopping this afternoon after we've worked out a strategy. I'll arrange an allowance.'

'Fine,' she said, feeling totally aggrieved, ramming her glasses up her nose defiantly as she turned on her heel. 'I just hope it's enough.'

It was more than enough. Philly surveyed the figure on the letter of authority Enid handed her with shock. Surely someone had made a mistake?

'I think there's one too many zeroes,' she suggested.

Enid glanced over, eyes peering through her bifocals. 'No, that's right. Now there are three boutiques listed where this authority is valid. They should be able to supply everything you need. If you have to go elsewhere, keep the receipts and you'll be reimbursed.'

'But this is a fortune.'

Enid smiled at the younger woman. 'He just wants you to look nice. It's important to him.'

'It's important to the deal, more like it,' she said, certain that nothing Damien thought about her would be personal. It would all relate to business.

The older woman's head tilted to one side.

'I think you'll find he's right. This deal's very important to the company and we have to do everything we can to ensure it comes off. I'm quite sure you'll feel more confident and more professional with a couple of new outfits and much more capable of holding your own. And I know Damien can seem a little tactless at times. But you mustn't take it too seriously. He simply hasn't had the same start most of us have had.'

If Philly hadn't heard his comment about losing his family earlier, she'd think Enid was mad. The guy was a multimillionaire, for goodness' sake, and here was someone practically feeling sorry for him.

Could Enid be right? The question plagued Philly's mind as she spent the next two hours searching for outfits suitable for meetings, possible cocktail parties and flash dinners in boutiques she'd only ever dreamed about entering before.

Was the early tragedy in his life the reason why he was so driven to succeed? So demanding of everyone around him? Was he trying to show the world he could make it on his own? Was that why he rode roughshod over everyone else's feelings—because his own had been so desperately and critically shattered at such a tender age?

Whoa! Next thing *she'd* be feeling sorry for him too. She didn't need that—not with the secret of last Saturday night playing on her mind.

And she couldn't afford to feel anything for Damien. If he'd thought he was easing her mind by declaring there was no way he'd be tempted to seduce her, he had another think coming.

He'd no doubt thought he was being considerate,

allaying a sweet innocent nobody's fears of seduction at the hands of her boss. When it was already too late for that. Much too late.

All he'd done was insult her. Making love with Cleopatra was one thing but making love with Philly Summers was never going to happen.

How reassuring! He'd made it clear that the man she couldn't stop fantasising about had her pegged around at the level of the woman least likely. How flattering—and yet here she was, supposed to feel relieved.

And all he'd done was to reinforce her resolve not to reveal her secret. Given his attitude he would be less impressed with the revelation. Clearly he would be embarrassed at the thought—probably even humiliated. Well, she would save them both that. She would forget it had ever happened. He need never know.

But if she became pregnant?

She shivered. She didn't want to go down that path. It was altogether too exciting and yet too terrifying. And the chances were so slim. How many couples got pregnant the first time they had unprotected sex anyway? It was hardly likely to be a consideration.

She sighed, fed up with both shopping and with the direction her thoughts were going. Spending two days in Damien's company would be bad enough. But to spend one night away—that could only be worse. She would have to do her best to remain cool, aloof and totally professional and with any luck he'd treat her with his usual professional disregard. Then in two weeks she'd have her period and there'd never be a reason she'd have to reveal a thing to him.

And in time she might even forget about what had happened in the boardroom, might stop thinking about the way his body had rippled in the slatted moonlight as he'd driven into her, the way he'd felt inside, possessing her.

Forget that night?

That was a laugh. There was no way she was ever going to be able to forget that.

She was late. The plane was due to take off in less than half an hour and she was nowhere to be seen. She couldn't have changed her mind—he'd arranged everything. The last time he'd spoken to her she'd even admitted that the live-in nurse Enid had organised was wonderful and that her mother was totally relaxed about the whole arrangement.

Not so Ms Summers. He could still see the nervous pinch to her lips, the strain in her face so evident whenever they'd discussed the upcoming trip. What was really bothering her? She couldn't be worried about him coming on to her. Hadn't he assured her this was purely a business trip? She wasn't his type for a start. Sure, she was great at her job but he had no more intention of seducing her than he would ask someone to marry him. It just wasn't going to happen.

In any event, he preferred his women lush, sexy and temporary, like that woman on Saturday night— her outfit accommodating, her attitude willing.

Though she'd proved far too temporary for his liking.

Who the hell was she anyway? Two days of scouring staff lists and making discreet enquiries had got him absolutely nowhere. His mystery woman remained that, a mystery. All he had was the memory of her, her fingers clutched behind his head, her tight breasts spilling out and her body open to him. His body responded to the images in his mind and he cursed low and rough as he helped himself to a cup of espresso.

He hadn't had enough of her, not by a long shot, but thinking about her now wasn't going to help him.

He lifted his head, scouring the airline club lounge once more as he emptied a stick of sugar into his cup but there was no sign of a sandy-coloured ponytail, no thick tortoiseshell glasses in evidence anywhere.

Damn, where the hell could she be?

A blonde in a pale green trouser suit approached the coffee station and he moved away to make room for her.

'I was wondering when you were going to get here.'

He swung back, coffee sloshing over the side of his cup. He steadied it with his other hand. His brain wasn't so easy to get a handle on. *Ms Summers?*

Sure enough it was her hazel eyes staring up at him, but they looked different. *She looked different.* He blinked.

'I booked one of the offices so we could go over the paperwork—just this way.'

He followed her into the small office, wondering just what had happened to his little brown mouse. She still smelled the same, the now familiar apricot scent wafting freshly in her wake. It was her looks that had changed. The long-line jacket sat over a fitted white shell top and seemingly floated behind her as she walked in matching trousers that weren't tight yet still hinted at womanly curves below.

Her hair, uncharacteristically worn down, was shoulder-length and feathered at the ends and it didn't look the colour of sand any more. It looked more like honey, honey sprinkled with crystals of sugar, the ends swishing and flicking with her motion. And what had she done with her glasses?

He was seated at the desk before he could talk. 'You look—different,' he said at last.

She smiled, almost as if self-conscious, as her gaze flicked over the outfit. 'I hope it's appropriate. I know business is a little more relaxed up in Queensland.'

He nodded his approval as his eyes slowly moved up her body. She fingered the ends of her hair and caught him looking. 'Oh, that. I was due for a cut so I let them talk me into something extra this time. But I didn't use your money. I paid for the hair myself.'

'What happened to your glasses?'

'Contact lenses. I lost one and had to get a new prescription made up. Still, I don't wear them as much as I should...' She hesitated. 'What's wrong?'

He realised he was staring. He coughed as he pulled his eyes away, lifting his laptop case to the table. 'Nothing,' he said with a shake of his head. 'We'll be boarding soon. We'd better get on with it.'

It was time well spent on the ground and in the air. By the time they'd arrived at Coolangatta Airport they'd thoroughly reviewed their potential client's specifications and finessed their plan of attack. Damien was feeling more and more confident even though he knew there was still a mountain of work ahead and a myriad of meetings with Palmcorp, their lawyers and financiers. But they could do it. He'd made the right choice in bringing her. They made a good team.

This was Damien at his best. In the large meeting room at Palmcorp's offices on the Gold Coast, Philly listened to his spiel, watched him charm, tease and manoeuvre the two directors and get them thinking his way. It was like watching a master at work.

No wonder he'd built his business to be the success it was. When he spoke he made you believe, the passion for his work and his products coming to the fore.

He held them in the palm of his hand.

It was a new side to Damien, one she hadn't witnessed before. Now his obsession with perfection, with driving his staff hard, made some sort of sense. He couldn't be that passionate about his business if the people who worked for him gave him less than their best.

His strong, deep voice flowed over the assembled group, his expressive hands adding gestures for emphasis where required, addressing them at their level, not preaching, not patronising, but taking every one of them with him. No one stopped him for questions or interrupted the flow. He was in his element. He was supreme.

It was impossible not to be impressed. And it wasn't just the way he spoke. The way he held himself and the way he looked had as much to do with it. He'd discarded his jacket and the fine white shirt only emphasised his olive skin and dark features.

He looked great in white. Even though his business shirt contrasted in a major way with the Roman armour he'd worn to the ball, both styles suited the man that he was.

She swallowed. He'd looked great in that outfit.

Then again, he'd looked great out of it. The way he'd discarded the armour, then the tunic, pulling it over his head and flinging it on the floor, the way his chest had expanded as her eyes had drunk him in, the way he'd stood next to her, waiting, anticipating…

Oh Lord, was she never going to get those pictures out of her head?

'Ms Summers?'

She came back to the meeting with a jolt to meet Damien's quizzical gaze. 'Is everything all right?'

She looked around in panic but the others all seemed busy helping themselves to the pots of filtered coffee and jugs of orange juice that had suddenly materialised from nowhere.

'You would like to handle the marketing perspective next up, I take it?'

'Oh yes, of course,' she said, her cheeks scorched and with confidence battling for dominance over visions of one gloriously near naked man. 'I was simply mentally preparing myself for the task. Excuse me, I think I'll get myself a juice.'

Her presentation sailed along, her earlier embarrassment soon forgotten as she got underway. She used the same basic format that she'd shown Damien at their meeting just a few weeks ago, expanding it to include additional detail for people less familiar with the company and the product. It seemed to go well and afterwards she fielded questions from the group before they all broke for a late lunch.

Damien sidled up alongside her as they were heading for the cars that would take them to the restaurant.

'Well done,' he said, bending down to whisper softly into her ear, his hand at her back. 'Excellent job.' He moved on, the curl of his breath against her skin rippling through her and tripping her heart-rate.

It took a deep breath to know how to respond as she battled to sort out the emotions vying for supremacy inside her. The employee side of her ego couldn't help but swell with pride that he considered she'd done her job well and his faith in her had been vindicated.

Yet another side of her that was already battered felt as if he had pressed hard on her most sensitive bruises. If only he had as much faith in her as a woman—if only he hadn't been so quick to write her off. Maybe there could have been a chance for something more to develop.

But what chance was there of that? They hadn't even shared a one-night stand. It had been more of a one shot wonder.

But by the time she'd realised that she should just smile and thank him he'd already turned away, thoroughly absorbed in a discussion of the finer points of European motor vehicle engineering.

She sighed. She'd missed her chance. Or she'd read much too much into his comments in the first place. Whatever, she really needed to relax more.

The afternoon didn't afford that. It was spent in more discussions and a tour of Palmcorp's offices before meetings with the finance and legal specialists that ran late. Again Damien steered the proceedings with skill and startling business acumen but did it in such a way that she could see the Palmcorp directors actually believing they were driving the process.

Businesswise, it was all proceeding very well. But with their early start it was a full-on day and all Philly wanted to do by the end was to go to her hotel room and enjoy a long hot soak. There was no time for that though, with a business dinner already arranged. At a pinch there'd be just enough time to shower and change.

Her room back at the hotel was spacious and elegant, luxury all the way, decorated in cool pastels with a wall of windows leading to a balcony, showcasing the brilliant blue of the ocean and the white sandy beach that stretched for miles to the north and south. A pity there was no time to enjoy it.

She had half an hour before she was to meet Damien in the lobby but she rang home before anything else. The nurse answered on the second ring, passing the phone over without hesitation. Her mother came on, her voice weak but with a bright note she hadn't heard for some time.

'How's it all going?' Philly asked her mother.

'I've been playing mah-jongg with Marjorie,' she said, 'and what's more I've been winning, so don't you worry about a thing. We're having a lovely time.'

She said goodbye and hung up on a smile, satisfied that she could at least relax on the domestic front. Tomorrow she'd be home and then, with any luck, she'd be able to relax on the Damien front too.

She'd done it again. Just like when she'd turned up in the airport lounge that morning, her appearance knocked him for a six. The dress she wore looked more like a coffee-coloured sheath, so hugging in the bodice that the tiny diamanté shoestring straps must be there purely for adornment, the floaty skirt constructed in separate panels wafting around her legs as she walked so that with every step the panels shifted slightly, revealing an ever changing and tantalising glimpse of flesh.

She'd put up her hair in a clasp but he could see the odd tendril floating free, bouncing as she moved towards him, and she'd done something with her face. Make-up? Whatever it was, her eyes looked bigger, her smile looked wider and her lips...

Red and lush, her lips looked like an invitation.

He swallowed. What had happened to his little brown mouse? Not that he didn't approve—she'd obviously made the most of the allowance he'd supplied for just that purpose—it was just that he hadn't been expecting such an amazing transformation.

Such an alluring transformation.

Dinner was fun. Stuart and Shayne Murchison, the directors of Palmcorp, were a dynamic pair in their late twenties, as attractive as they were successful. Both shared the same tanned good looks, with blue eyes and hair bleached by too much sun and surf from the regular iron-man competitions they took part in, competing as much against each other as the clock.

They were also very good hosts, treating their guests to a fabulous seafood dinner on a restaurant terrace overlooking the beach, entertaining them with anecdotes from their long history of competitions and all the while arguing incessantly as to who was the fastest swimmer or could catch the best waves.

'So why aren't either of you married?' she asked, partly for fun, partly curious that neither of the men had been snapped up.

'Ah, that's easy,' said Stuart.

'No one's ever been able to swim fast enough to catch us,' finished Shayne, and the brothers laughed as if it was an all too well practised line.

'But,' Stuart offered, his eyes glinting wickedly at Philly's, 'that doesn't mean we're not still looking.'

As she laughed her way with them Philly felt the tension of the last few days slipping away. She hadn't enjoyed herself so much for ages. Knowing her mother was being well taken care of, and in her new clothes under the sails of a sunny terrace just a stone's throw from the sparkling blue ocean, she felt a new woman. Certainly to be the only woman at a table of such good-looking men was a novelty. Maybe it wasn't such a bad idea coming on this trip after all.

All three men turned heads in the restaurant, making her the object of envy from the waitresses and plenty of the guests besides, but even though all were good-looking there was no argument in Philly's mind as to just which man dominated the proceedings. The brothers were ultrafit and no weaklings, yet Damien, all dark brooding looks and latent power inherent in his every move, dwarfed them with his sheer presence.

Her eyes settled on him now as he quietly allowed the brothers full rein at being hosts. Only the scowl between his dark brows betrayed him. No doubt he'd be thinking about the meetings to come, wheels spinning as he developed plans and devised tactics to close the deal.

He turned suddenly and snagged her eyes with a look that sparked and flared and she jerked her head away sharply, feeling caught out, not understanding the sudden aggression in his eyes and trying to focus back on the conversation with a face that bore the heat from his gaze.

'Tell me about your name.' Stuart Murchison leaned closer, clearly oblivious to her discomfiture, one arm at the back of her chair, his body turned to hers, his other hand swirling what was left of his glass of premium Hunter Valley shiraz. 'Philly. That's so unusual. There must be a story behind it.'

Damien bristled as he glared at Stuart's back. Okay, so the dinner had gone well, the whole day had gone well, and with a pinch of luck tomorrow Palmcorp would sign on the dotted line, but that didn't mean his assistant was up for grabs. She wasn't part of the deal. Sure, he'd wanted her to look presentable, had even supplied her with the funds to do so. But did she have to have done it quite so successfully?

He stirred his coffee longer than was absolutely necessary and discarded his spoon with a solid clink. The sooner this night ended the better.

Alongside him, Philly smiled in response to Stuart's question and took a sip of her mineral water.

'This is probably going to sound really silly…'

'Of course it won't,' said Stuart, stroking her shoulder, 'you can tell us.'

Damien resisted the urge to growl, instead focusing on Philly's response.

She cradled the glass between her two hands on the table and smiled. 'Okay then. My parents wanted to give their children names that were a bit different. They decided on the names of cities that they liked the sound of.' She looked from the face of one brother to the other. 'Oh, gosh, that does sound weird, doesn't it, especially seeing no one but my mother calls me Philadelphia anyway. It always gets shortened to Philly.'

'Not at all,' Shayne said, shaking his head. Stuart put down his glass. 'So they named you Philadelphia?' He nodded. 'Yeah, I like it. So what did your folks call the other kids—Melbourne—Paris—Constantinople?'

Even from where he was sitting Damien sensed the change in her as she ignored the light-hearted banter, her eyes focusing on the glass between her hands. 'There was only one other. My kid brother. They named him Montreal.'

'Montreal. That's unusual,' said Stuart.

'I know.' She smiled softly, letting her head fall to one side. 'He hated it so we call him—' She hesitated, suddenly biting down on her bottom lip. 'We used to call him Monty instead.'

There was a quiet resonance in her words that went way beyond what was spoken.

'What happened to him?' Damien asked softly, before he'd realised he'd even put voice to his question.

Her eyes were fixed on the glass, her thumbs stroking away the condensation forming and reforming on the outside.

'He was a pilot, flying home for the weekend with Annelise, his wife, to show off their new baby son. They'd named him after our father—he died ten years ago and mum was so proud that they'd named the baby after him. She couldn't wait to meet her first grandchild.' She took a breath, as if unwilling to give voice to what came next for fear it would be true.

'There was a storm *en route* and something went wrong; they think a lightning strike took out the electrical system.' She shrugged. 'Whatever. The plane crashed and they all…every one of them. They all died.' Her voice dropped to a whisper. 'Thomas was just ten days old.'

Forces shifted inside him as the silence that followed blanketed the table. The quiet emotion of her words betrayed a feeling he recognised, a feeling buried deep inside.

But it was a feeling he didn't want to be reminded of. He didn't want to pull it out and examine what it meant. It was better off left exactly where it was.

Philly looked up at the faces around the table. 'Oh, I'm sorry, you didn't want to hear all that. Please forgive me.'

Stuart was the first to react. His arm shifted from the chair back to around her shoulders and he gave her a squeeze, putting his wineglass down so he could cover her hands in his. 'Don't apologise,' he said softly. 'There's absolutely no need.'

She smiled up at him, her lashes moist, eyes glistening. 'Thank you, Stuart.'

'Call me Stu,' he said, his voice low and sympathetic. 'All my friends do.'

Her smile widened. 'Thank you, Stu.'

Damien pushed himself out of his chair. 'Time to call it a night. Thank you, gentlemen. We'll see ourselves back to the hotel.'

Philly looked up, surprised by his sudden action. 'Oh, right. Okay.'

She made a move to stand but Stuart placed an ironman fist over her arm, pinning her to the chair. 'It's still early,' he said, his eyes fixed on Philly but the tone of his words aimed directly at Damien. 'Maybe Philly would like to see a little more of the Gold Coast entertainment.'

His eyes softened. 'Would you like that, Philly? Do you like to dance?'

'Um, yes, actually,' she said, her voice wavering. 'I do.'

He turned to Damien triumphantly. 'So that's settled, then. Sorry you don't feel up to joining us, Damien, but we'll see you tomorrow morning at the office. And don't worry, we'll look after Philly for you.'

Damien battled with the urge to rearrange one smug face, but he wasn't about to undo all the goodwill they'd built up today. Then again, he wasn't about to be out-manoeuvred either.

He dredged up a laugh, as if he was enjoying the banter, and schooled his voice to sound civilised while inside him his heartbeat pounded like jungle drums. 'Another time, perhaps. Sorry to disappoint you, but Ms Summers and I have some important details to go over tonight. I'm sure you understand.'

With that he placed a firm hand under her elbow and levered her from her chair. Stuart was left with no choice but to remove his hand from her arm though he made no pretence that he was happy about it.

'Good night, gentlemen. I look forward to furthering our discussions in the morning.'

He steered Philly out of the restaurant and into a waiting taxi without saying another word.

'What was that all about?'

She was sick of the silent treatment, sick of the brooding male who had sprawled over the taxi seat like a despot, arrogant limbs taking up space as if he owned it, sick of the way he'd frog-marched her to her door like a prisoner to be locked in for the night.

As his silence continued her anger grew and grew, simmering away, fuelled by the heat he was giving off with his black mood.

'What was what all about?'

'Don't give me that,' she said as she inserted her card key into the reader. 'You acted like some caveman back there at the restaurant.'

Down the corridor the lift doors binged open, spilling a load of camera-wielding tourists into the hallway.

The lock clicked open. Damien grabbed the handle and turned. 'Inside,' he said, half shoving her across the threshold, closing the door behind them.

'Excuse me,' she said, wheeling around to face him, hands on hips. 'What the hell do you think you're doing now?'

'Keeping our private business just that. Private. There's no need to share it with a busload of tourists.'

'Well, don't make yourself comfortable then because what I have to say to you will only take a moment. You had no right to come on like that back there.'

'I'm your boss. I had every right.'

'Is that so? Then where's this important work we need to go over then? You never said anything about it before. You made that up.'

'We have important meetings tomorrow and you know it.'

'Yes, with people you did your best to completely alienate tonight. What on earth were you thinking?'

'I was thinking I brought you up here to work with me, not to flirt with the customers.'

Her mouth fell open in disbelief. 'I wasn't flirting!'

'Come on. You had *Stu-baby* draped all over you like a gorilla.'

'He was being sympathetic, that's all.'

'Sympathetic? Is that what you call it when someone's angling to get into your pants?'

'How dare you?' The crack of her palm against his cheek was as loud as it was satisfying. Her victory was short-lived though as he snared her still open hand in one swift-moving fist. His other hand stroked the region, a red weal already brightening under his fingers.

'You deserved that.' She spat the words out over a gasping breath, refusing to give in to her first instinct to apologise.

He looked down at her, dark fire burning in his eyes, his breathing strangely calm under the circumstances. 'And this,' he said, pulling on her wrist so that she collided full length with him, 'is what you deserve.'

Still half off balance, she felt his arm surround her and haul her tightly against him as his head dipped lower. Panic, outrage and sheer bliss all welled within her as his lips meshed with hers; panic that he would somehow recognise her as the woman he'd made love to on Saturday night; outrage that he could treat her this way, and sheer unadulterated bliss that he had.

Since their encounter at the ball she'd dreamed of nothing else but to be in Damien's arms once more. Those dreams had ended in disappointed awakenings and frustrated tomorrows. But now he was here, really here, holding her, *kissing her* and it was no dream.

Her thin sand-washed satin dress might not have been there. She could feel all of him, the length of him, the heat of him, searing her through the fine fabric.

He let go of her wrist and his hand went behind her head, drawing her closer, holding her firm and somewhere his anger turned into something else. It was desire she could feel from him now, a hot, urgent thing that was as tangible as the flesh beneath her hands and it called to her, tempting her, insisting she give herself up to it.

Why shouldn't she?

It would be so easy.

She knew the pleasure she'd find. She'd only had a sample of what he had to offer, but there was no doubt there was so much more that she'd like to experience. Why should it matter if she did?

But how could she?

Things were complicated between them already. Already there were secrets. Already there was too much to explain. This wasn't going to help.

Besides, he didn't want her. He'd made that perfectly plain when he'd set the boundaries for this trip. What was happening now had more to do with his competitive nature and showing her who was boss than any real interest he had in Philly Summers. Because he'd made it perfectly clear that he had none.

And that was the killer punch. If she'd thought for a moment that he felt something for her other than pure animal lust, if she thought she had something else going for her in his eyes other than simply being available, then yes, she'd like nothing more than to give herself up to the pleasures he promised.

But this was no fancy dress ball where he had no idea of her identity. This was no masquerade. Here there was no avoidance of the truth. He'd never wanted her and, whatever his motives, he didn't really want her now.

This was simply wrong.

His hands slipped to her shoulders, sliding her thin straps away. She gasped as his hands followed the curve of her shoulders, around to the front, lower, capturing her breasts, thumbs hooking in her bodice top, easing it lower.

Her hands found his chest as she dragged her face away from his. She pushed but his hands caught her and pulled her back. She pushed again, harder, turning her face so that he couldn't kiss her.

'No,' she said, her breath choppy. 'Stop this.'

His mouth was at her neck, cajoling, insisting and panic gripped her.

'*No!*' she yelled. 'Just because you bought these clothes don't assume you own what's in them.'

'The clothes are yours,' he muttered, ignoring her jibe, his breath hot and persuasive against her skin. 'Keep them.'

She squeezed her eyes shut, praying for strength.

'You promised!'

His head lifted but he didn't let go. 'What did I promise?'

'Not to maul me. You promised me there was no chance you would seduce me on this trip. You made it perfectly clear there was not a snowball's chance in hell—remember? So let me go—now.'

He had promised, he remembered. Why the hell had he done that?

His arms slackened their grip around her and she eased herself away, hitching up her shoulder straps before flicking back her hair with her fingers. Her face was flushed, her lips bruised and swollen from his attention and he ached to take her back into his arms and finish what he'd begun.

He'd made that promise to someone else, though— someone else who wore ill-fitting brown suits and glasses that wouldn't be out of place on a welder. He hadn't made that guarantee to the woman standing in front of him. He would have been mad to have done that.

'I think you should leave,' she said, not moving, clutching her arms over her chest like a shield. 'Now.'

He took a deep breath. He would go. After all, he had promised.

But he definitely wouldn't make that mistake again.

CHAPTER SIX

CHRISTMAS came early to the Summers' household.

Five mornings before the big day, Philly clutched the white stick, hand shaking, eyes disbelieving, mind unable to comprehend. She looked again at the instructions, reading the last section twice over until she was sure she had it clear in her mind, then she looked back at the stick.

There was no mistake.

She had read it right.

She was pregnant.

Elation zipped through her. She'd done it! She was carrying a child. Having a baby was no longer just a dream, just a hope. It was now a reality. And in less than forty weeks, all going well, she would hold that baby in her arms. And her mother would hold her grandchild.

Please God it wouldn't be too late for it to make a difference.

But it couldn't be too late. It was a miracle. She was having a baby.

Her baby.

Elation suddenly gave way to another emotion.

Dread.

This wasn't just her baby. It was Damien's too.

Guilt gripped her heart, squeezing it as tight as the instructions now crumpled within her fist as her body swayed into the bathroom vanity unit, knocking the soap dish to the floor.

This was not some IVF pregnancy, where the sperm had been donated with the intention and hopes of furnishing someone with a child anonymously. This child's father was no phantom, no unnamed donor whose chosen part in conceiving a child was over.

This child's father was Damien DeLuca, about as far from a phantom as ice was from the sun. And he would have to be told.

Oh, he wouldn't like it. The self-confessed career bachelor and man about town was hardly likely to be excited at the prospect of discovering he was to be a father. But if he was angry about it he could hardly blame her. Neither of them had given a moment's thought to protection that night. Sure, she was the one who was pregnant, but he wasn't exactly the innocent party in all this.

Yet none of that really mattered. There was no question that she had to tell him. It wouldn't be right or fair to deny Damien the existence of his own child, just as it would be wrong to prevent that child from knowing the identity of its father.

She gazed unseeing into the mirror. And maybe, once he knew, just maybe there was a sliver of possibility that he might even care…

She shook her head, shaking out the wistful dreams and hopes. She was having a baby—wasn't that enough?

Damien would just have to deal with it, just as she would. First though, she had to tell him.

She hauled herself upright and away from the vanity. It was just as well the office was closing over Christmas. She had two weeks off to spend with her mother. She'd use the time well, see a doctor, get confirmation of her home pregnancy test result and obtain some advice about the best time to tell her mother.

'Philly?' Her mother's voice came muted from outside the door. 'Are you all right? I thought I heard something crash.'

She looked around her and saw the soap dish, now lying shattered in pieces on the floor. She hadn't even noticed. 'I'm fine,' she called back. 'Just clumsy today.'

Her mother would be delighted when she discovered why. She stooped to pick up the largest pieces and tried to quell a sudden pang of remorse. She wouldn't be judgmental—her mother wasn't like that—but she'd be curious all the same and maybe just a tiny bit sad that there was no boyfriend or husband on the scene. She'd wanted to see Philly settled down after all.

But she'd considered that same scenario when she'd applied to undergo IVF treatment. She'd known that it would still be worth it, that any disappointment would be short lived in the joy that a new baby brought, especially when that baby meant so much.

As for telling Damien? She had to tell him as soon as possible. It had been one thing to keep her secret to herself when there was no chance of him ever finding out. But now there was no way. The product of that secret would soon betray her anyway.

As soon as the doctors had confirmed the pregnancy. The first chance she had, she would tell him.

CHAPTER SEVEN

'ENID!' Where was that woman? *'Enid!'*

Enid appeared at his office doorway, pen and blue folder at the ready.

'You rang?' she asked, one eyebrow skewed north.

He gritted his teeth. He never liked it when she took that tone. Having a PA who knew too much about you was a positive drawback at times.

'Where the hell have you been?'

'Completing the papers you asked me to fax the last time you bellowed at me, not five minutes ago. Not to mention,' she added before he had a chance to respond, 'sorting out two weeks worth of mail you demanded barely five minutes before that. And answering the phone in between—you did ask me to take even your direct line calls for today. And thank you for asking, I had a wonderful Christmas holiday. At least, I imagine that's why you demanded my presence this time?'

For a moment he was speechless. 'Well, good for you,' he replied with a snarl, wondering just why the hell he had wanted to see her.

'And Switzerland?' she continued, her eyes narrowing as if she was peering right into his soul. 'How was the skiing this year? Normally you come back a little more relaxed after your break.'

'Fine,' he snapped, drumming his fingers on the table while he tried to forget all about his failure of a holiday and remember what he wanted Enid for. 'Switzerland was fine.'

'Wonderful,' said Enid in a tone that said pigs could fly. 'Then maybe you'd like to go over what's in your diary for today.'

His head snapped up. That was it. 'Only if you've finished discussing my social calendar,' he retorted. 'My diary *is* why I asked you here in the first place.'

'I see,' said Enid, clearly nonplussed. 'Only you never said.' She flipped open the folder in her hands. 'First up at nine, you have an hour long meeting with Philly about the roll out of the new campaign, after which...'

He jerked upright and out of his chair at the sound of that name, turning to the window as Enid's voice droned on in the background listing today's appointments.

Philly. What was it about her that made him so unsettled? How did she do that? He glanced down at his watch as Enid's unheeded dialogue tailed off. Eight-thirty. She'd be here in half an hour. Barely any time at all. So why did thirty minutes suddenly seem so long?

Philly wondered if this was how morning sickness felt. It was still only early in her pregnancy, but she'd been fine up until now, finding it difficult to believe she really was pregnant, even after her doctor's confirmation and referral to a specialist. She had felt so unchanged, so utterly well.

Until today. Her gut churned, her legs felt less solid than the rice pudding she'd made for her mother last night and it had nothing to do with the motion of the train wending its way closer to Melbourne's city centre, closer to making her announcement to Damien. She knew she couldn't put it off. She knew she'd have to tell him some time. But she just wasn't at all confident she could do this today.

But neither could she delay it. The longer she did that, the harder it would be.

The train stopped, mid station. Heads lifted from newspapers and novels, knitting needles stopped clacking and fifty heads swivelled around, searching for some explanation for the delay. The speakers crackled into life with the grim news. A minor derailment ahead and a delay of at least an hour. Fifty disgruntled passengers gave a collective groan, giving up any hopes of an early start, and pulled out mobile phones to relay the news before turning their attention resignedly back to their activities.

At least an hour. Another hour to think about what she had to do. Another hour for her insides to rebel. It was the last thing she needed today. She glanced at her watch, realising she wouldn't be at work anywhere close to being in time for her meeting with Damien and rummaged in her handbag for her own mobile phone. At least she could let him know she'd be late.

Damien knew the moment she arrived. Standing with his hands in pockets, gazing out over the view of the city, he'd heard the soft ping of the lift bell and the whoosh of the doors and he'd known instinctively that she was finally here. He was sure those were her hurried footsteps tearing along the plush careting, and already he could even imagine the scent of apricots drifting along the corridor.

Funny how he couldn't get that scent out of his

head. Even in the chalet in Klosters, surrounded by beautiful women, perfumed and perfectly made-up and offering the ultimate *après-ski* experience, it had been the faint scent of apricots that had haunted his dreams. For someone who'd almost made a career of studying the effects of different perfumes on women, enjoying the effects of perfume on them, suddenly they no longer appealed. They were all too heavy, too sickly, too cloying.

It hadn't been a good holiday. Instead of being relaxed he'd had too much time to think. And there were two women he couldn't get out of his mind. One was a woman who'd let him make sweet love to her and then disappeared off the face of the earth, a woman who defied every attempt of his to track her down.

The other was a paradox, a strange mixture of innocence but with a hidden core, a centre he was finding more beguiling as the layers came off. And when he'd wanted her, she'd turned him down flat.

No one had ever done that before.

Two women, two totally unsatisfactory experiences. No wonder he was having trouble sleeping.

And now one of them couldn't even make it into work on time. Things were going to have to change around here.

He heard her brief greeting to Enid and the older woman's reply, followed by a low, 'He's waiting for you. Better go straight in.' It sounded to Damien like a warning. *Damned right.*

He waited until he could hear her footfall near his door, her breath rapid but soft, as if she was trying not to let on she was worried. He turned.

'You're late!'

'I'm sorry, but—'

'Our meeting was for nine o'clock. It's now closer to ten.'

'I phoned you…Enid—'

'You don't work for Enid. You work for me. When you can be bothered to turn up.'

'That's not fair—'

Her protest was cut off with a violent slash of his hand through the air that ended with a slam of his open palm on the desk.

'Are these the sort of hours you expect to be paid for? Because there's no place for freeloaders in this organisation.'

'I can't help it if the trains are late.'

'It's your job to get to work on time. Period. If the trains can't get you here on time, find a reliable form of transport.'

'I'll work through lunch. I'll make it up.'

'Damned right you will.'

'Fine,' she said with a sniff, pulling herself upright that way she did as if it added inches. 'At least we agree on something.'

He stopped, the wind taken out of his sails as soon as she'd stopped defending herself. His pause gave him his first chance to really look at her. Her soft linen shift fitted her well without being tight, its pastel tones cool and perfect for summer. By contrast her hazel eyes were blazing but instead of her face glowing red she looked so pale, her skin almost translucent.

'Are you okay?'

Something flared, bright and potent in her eyes, before it was just as quickly extinguished. 'Perfectly well.'

'It's just that you look a bit…washed out.'

Could he tell? Was it that obvious?

'Er, I ran all the way from the station and…' She licked her lips. She'd been going to wait until after their discussion of the roll out of the new campaign, but maybe this was as good a time as any. It might serve to wipe that pompous look off his face.

He watched her. 'And?' he prompted.

'And I'm pregnant.'

Stunned silence met her announcement. But only for a few moments. Then all hell broke loose.

'You're *what?*'

'I'm pregnant.' Actually, now that she'd said it out loud, she felt pretty good. It was good to say it. It was good to tell someone who didn't have the title of doctor before their name. A smile made its way to her lips as her hand rested over her tummy. 'I'm having a baby.'

His eyes followed the movement of her hand but there was no accompanying smile. In fact the way his lip curled made him look positively hostile.

'How the hell did that happen?'

She shrugged, still unable to stop smiling. That smug look of his was nowhere to be seen. 'The usual way.' She thought about that for a second more, enjoying the experience of turning the tables on him. 'Or not so usual, I gather.'

He grunted, clearly unimpressed, his anger wrapped around him like a shroud. 'I didn't pick you for being careless. I certainly hope you're more responsible when you're at work.'

'*I* was careless? Oh, that's rich, coming from y—'

'If you don't mind,' his terse words interjected,

'we're supposed to be talking about the campaign—
that is, if you're up to it.'

'Of course I'm up to it. But Damien, I need to tell
you that—'

His body jerked up in his seat. 'That what? You're
not thinking of leaving the company, are you? That
would be damned inconvenient after promoting you.
I'm relying on you to see this new campaign through.'

'No, nothing like that. Not unless you think I
should.'

'Why would I think that?'

'Well, it's just that…'

She paused, aware of a disturbance down the hall
which was rapidly escalating into a commotion—
someone was arguing with Enid. A moment later the
door was flung wide open.

Her mouth dropped open as her ex-fiancé, carrying
a large bunch of stem roses and a bottle of champagne, burst in with Enid close on his heels.

'Excuse me, Mr Chalmers, you can't go in there.'

'Relax,' Bryce crooned as he lit up one of his dazzling smiles. 'I'm sure whoever this is—' he nodded
dismissively towards Damien '—will excuse us.
Philly and I have important business to discuss.'

'Mr Chalmers, would you please leave. This is not
Ms Summers's office.'

'Don't worry, Enid.' Damien took a step back as
he lowered himself into his chair, sensing an opportunity to learn more about the secret life of Philly.
First pregnant, now this character, whom one could
only assume to be the father. Was he the reason she'd
knocked back Damien's advances at the Gold Coast?

He felt himself bristling at the thought.

Bryce completely disregarded everyone's presence

but Philly's, sitting himself down on the desk opposite her. She made an attempt to get up but he pushed her back down, thrusting the bunch of flowers into her lap. 'For you, sweetheart, and hey, you're looking better than ever.' He leaned over and pecked her on her still open lips before he began removing the foil from the top of the champagne bottle.

Philly stared blankly at the flowers but had finally found her voice. 'Bryce—what's going on? What are you doing here?'

'I was going to surprise you when you got home but I thought it would be much more fun to whisk you away from here to a nice romantic restaurant some place. You've moved up in the world. Last time I visited you in here you were on a lower floor. Sam—someone-or-other told me where to find you.'

Damien made a mental note to have a quiet word with Sam about company security while he thought about grinding Bryce's face into the carpet for stealing that kiss. But then why would she be so shocked about her child's father turning up—unless they'd broken up after the baby had been conceived? His little brown mouse had more layers than the DeLuca Tower.

'Bryce, why are you here? This doesn't make sense.'

The visitor ignored her protest and, despite the early hour, levered out the cork, setting it free with a loud pop, and pouring the wine into two glasses he'd extracted from his pocket. He handed her one and took a swig from the other.

Then he turned and locked his baby-blue eyes on her, a lock of his blonde hair escaping from under the designer sunglasses perched on his head.

'Then let's go make sense somewhere private,' he said. 'Away from all these cronies.'

Damien couldn't keep silent any more—whoever this guy was, there was no way he'd let Philly leave while he was paying her salary.

'She's not going anywhere with you.'

Bryce turned, obviously displeased to find the company he'd so readily dismissed hadn't instantaneously vaporised.

'Excuse me, this *is* a private conversation.'

Enid tut-tutted at the door and put her fists on her hips.

'Imagine that, and we all thought it was *you* interrupting a private conversation.'

Bryce smiled a false smile that got no further than his bared teeth. 'I appreciate your loyalty to Philly. It's very…touching. But she's safe with me. Aren't you, Philly?'

Philly took a long look at Bryce as she put her untouched glass on the desk. Even in the midst of her surprise, when he'd first walked in she had been blown away with how good-looking he was, with his tanned skin, blue eyes and blonde hair. For just a while there she'd felt this huge sense of loss—she'd loved and lost this perfect specimen.

But then she'd noticed the way he treated people, the way he rode roughshod over anyone who didn't serve a purpose to him, and the way he'd assumed she would fall into his arms without a thought to ask her what she wanted.

Why had she put up with him for all that time? She must have been so desperate to have a child it had completely blinkered her view. But the shutters were off now and there was no way he was barging his way back into her life.

'Philly?' Bryce prompted.

She looked around Bryce to where Damien was sitting poised, ready to pounce. With his face like thunder, he looked as if he was prepared to tear Bryce limb from limb. Standing behind her at the door, Enid looked more than ready to deputise.

It was empowering having them both here for moral support. And comforting. Only this was something she'd have to deal with herself. Besides which, if she was going to have to explain her pregnancy to Bryce it would be better not to have Damien around to complicate matters.

She exhaled on a long sigh before glancing up to Damien and Enid. 'I'm sorry, I don't know what's going on, but if you'd give me just a moment to sort this out? I appreciate your support but we need a little privacy. If you don't mind, we'll continue this in my office. It won't take long.'

Enid and Damien looked at each other, as if neither was prepared to be the first to leave.

'You're sure?' Damien asked.

'I'm sure.'

'Then you stay here. I'll be right outside if you need.'

She smiled. 'Thanks.' Their eyes met again and locked. *It'll be okay*, they seemed to be saying. Warmth spiralled through her, touching her in places only he seemed to be able to reach. It was a good feeling.

'Right!' Bryce announced, clapping his hands and jolting her out of her mood. 'You've both been a wonderful audience but the show's over. Allow me to show you the door.'

Damien stood, visibly bristling even as Enid made for a quick exit. Bryce stopped dead in his tracks. 'Come on,' he urged, sounding less cocky, 'you heard the lady. We'd appreciate a little privacy.'

From her chair Philly could tell Damien was itching to do something—she didn't know what, but he looked as tight as a drum. His dark eyes took on the character of petrified wood—the hardness of stone, polished and glinting.

The contrast between the men hit her then. There was Bryce, elegant as always in his superfine wool suit and with his charming good looks, but soft on the inside. And there was Damien, rock solid, staring him down, exuding more masculine power in those eyes than Bryce owned in his entire body.

A breath caught in her throat as a thrill descended her spine.

He was defending her!

Something warm and luxurious enveloped her just as effectively as if Damien had wrapped his arms around her. She had a champion. Damien would look after her. She knew it just as surely as she knew to draw her next breath and that knowledge gave her strength.

He must care for her—just a little, at least. Maybe one day he could care for them both…

A movement caught her eye and she realised it was Bryce's Adam's apple jerking up and down.

Damien raised his chin fractionally and repeated, 'I'll be right outside,' before he turned on his heel and left the room.

A moment later Bryce closed the door behind them.

He shrugged. 'Well, he's certainly uptight about something. Why don't we just clear out of this nuthouse altogether? Philly, grab your jacket and bag, we may as well hit the road and find that restaurant, even if it is still early.'

She leaned back in her chair. Already he was barking orders at her and he'd only reappeared in her life barely ten minutes ago. What would it be like if she took him back? Not that that was on the cards once he heard her news.

'We don't need a restaurant. We can talk here. What I have to say isn't going to be any more palatable when accompanied with fine food and wine.'

He came back around the desk and reached for her hands. 'Aww. Come on, Philly. Can't you let bygones be bygones? I made a mistake, pure and simple. Everyone does. But I'll make it up to you.'

She shook her head slowly. 'Bryce, I honestly don't think…'

'Listen, I would never have left you if Muriel hadn't told me she was pregnant. And she lied to me. It was never my baby! She tricked me into moving in with her. It's all her fault.'

'You were having an *affair* with her for at least a year before that happened. Or am I supposed to conveniently forget about that?'

Bryce shook his head, looking wounded. 'But this is what you wanted. When you rang and told me you'd do anything to get me back, you weren't worried about a meaningless little fling then.'

She bowed her head. It was true. In those first few days after Bryce had left she had wanted nothing more than for him to come back to her. She'd even been willing to overlook his straying ways if only he'd soothe the huge sense of rejection he'd left her with. And, after a great deal of hand-wringing, she'd swallowed what little pride she had left and called him on his mobile phone, pleading with him to come back to her.

Funny, but she couldn't remember him saying that he'd see how it went with Muriel and get back to her if it didn't work out. As far as she could recall, his parting words had been, '*Get a life*'.

She smiled inwardly at the words. How was Bryce going to feel when he found out she'd done just that?

'That was a long time ago. I don't think I could forget about it so easily now.'

'It's all in the past. Can't we move on?'

She looked at him for a moment. Muriel must have put him through the wringer. Now that she was over the shock of seeing him again, close up she could see the tell-tale signs of strain around his eyes. His face had a more pinched look than she remembered.

He was obviously hurting and he'd come to her. Once she might have fallen for his hangdog expression. But no longer.

'I have moved on. I don't want to go back.'

He looked up. 'You're seeing someone else then?'

Philly laughed. The way he'd so confidently just waltzed in and assumed she was available and waiting for him to come back into her life—and now he looked almost worried.

'Well, not exactly—'

Relief took over his features.

'So why can't you just give me one more chance?'

'Even if I did, what's to stop you having another affair?'

'No, not a chance. I've learnt my lesson. I'll stick with the tried and true.'

Raising her eyebrows, she could barely manage a response to that back-handed compliment. 'Gee, thanks, that makes me sound special.'

'You are special, Philly. I shouldn't need to tell you. You're sweet, you're clever and you love me. What more could I ask?'

Philly knew full well that whatever her supposed attributes he'd wandered before while he had her love. What would stop him now that he didn't?

'Look, it just won't work—not now.'

'Because you won't forgive me?'

For a moment the temptation to tell him she was pregnant was overwhelming. After all, this guy had featured large for over two years of her life. She was used to sharing secrets and life stories with him. Though that was before…

Now he was merely part of her history. There was really no reason to tell him about the baby at all. Sure he wouldn't want her once he found out about the baby, but she needed him to understand she didn't want him anyway.

'No. Because you were wrong. I don't love you any more. I'm not convinced I ever did. It's taken me a while, but I'm getting my life together. I want it to stay that way. There's no place in my life for you now.'

His face stilled momentarily before a slight tic started up under his right eye.

'You're joking, right?' He tried to smile, but the tic got in the way, jerking up the side of his lip.

'I'm joking, wrong.'

Putting his head down, he paced a few steps around

the office. Suddenly he stopped and looked up at her. 'Then what am I expected to do? I gave up my flat when I moved in with Muriel. I've got nowhere to go.'

Philly almost laughed, until she realised he was serious. 'Excuse me, but I don't think that's my problem.'

His face took a bitter twist as his tic worked overtime.

'Then think again, sweetheart. I'm moving in with you tonight.'

Suddenly she needed to get out of there—and fast. For someone who'd up until today had an enviable absence of morning sickness she felt pretty close to losing everything she'd managed to keep down in the last six weeks and more.

'Excuse me—' She rushed for the door and pulled it open, only to almost trip over the huddled form of Enid, who was trying to look inconspicuous watering the pot-plants just outside the door. Damien stopped his pacing in the waiting area beyond and looked up at her, the storm in his eyes giving way fractionally to concern. For a moment as their eyes met in the confusion she forgot her nausea completely. But only for a moment. Then she felt the surge inside her once more and she rushed past Enid into the rest-rooms beyond.

'What the hell's going on out there?' Bryce called. 'Philly, where are you?'

'I'll go see how she is,' Enid volunteered, following.

'The hell you will. I'll go!' asserted Bryce, pushing his way into the bathroom.

Almost immediately he wavered, turning back at the sounds of her distress, his face taking on a noticeably green tinge. 'Aah, I don't think she's very well.'

Enid scowled at him. 'A lot you seem to care.'

Damien joined them outside the door. 'You idiot. She's probably feeling sick enough with the baby coming without you upsetting her.'

'I've explained that,' Bryce stated. 'It wasn't my…'

There was silence for a few seconds until Philly wobbled to the door, looking washed out and holding a damp paper towel to her face. 'Phew, that was too close. Panic over.'

Damien held out his arm, questions in his eyes. 'Lean on me. Come and sit down.'

She took his arm, avoiding the questions and letting herself sink her weight gratefully against him as he led her down to the more comfortable chairs in the waiting room.

'You need a nice cup of tea,' suggested Enid, disappearing into the small kitchenette to put the kettle on.

Bryce trailed them down the hall, all the time his eyes dashing between Philly and Damien and back again before finally settling around the region of Philly's still flat abdomen as she reclined into an armchair. His tongue darted out and flicked around his lips nervously.

'Um. What's going on?'

She looked up at him, her eyes weary. 'Bryce, there's no place for you back in my life. I wasn't going to tell you because it's actually none of your business, but I'm pregnant.'

He looked around, panic evident in his eyes. 'But—you can't be. We haven't—I always used—It's been months!'

'Oh, don't worry,' she said, 'I never said it was yours.'

'Then who the hell have you been sleeping with?'

Damien couldn't stay quiet any longer. He didn't have any idea how this baby had been conceived, but he sure as hell was happy it had nothing to do with Bryce. 'You've got to be joking! Surely you don't expect Philly to answer that question,' he snapped.

'I want to know. The minute my back is turned, she goes and gets herself pregnant. Whose is it?'

'Philly told you, it's none of your business. Maybe it's about time you were thinking about leaving again—this time for good.'

Bryce looked around and threw Damien a hateful expression. 'Why don't you just stay out of this?' he snapped, before his eyes suddenly narrowed. 'Hang on…'

He looked from Philly's face to Damien's and back again. Damien glared right back.

'Damien's right,' she said. 'You should go.'

Bryce's searching gaze focused once more on Philly, his lip curling. 'It's his baby, isn't it? You probably couldn't wait for me to be out of the picture. In fact, it was probably going on before I left. That's what you're doing up on this swank floor. You earned your promotion on your back. Go on—deny it.'

Philly squeezed her eyes shut and wished she could do the same for her ears. This couldn't be happening.

'Why deny it?' said Damien, his voice heavy with anger, his hands curling into fists. 'It is my baby.'

Philly's heart missed a beat as her eyes snapped open.

'Damien…'

'So understand me when I say,' continued Damien as he forced Bryce to the lifts without touching him but by his sheer physical presence. 'You stay away from Philly. I never want you to contact her again. And I don't want to see your face around here either. Got that?'

The lift doors behind Bryce slid open. For a moment it looked as if he was trying to make a last-ditch attempt. His chest puffed out and his red cheeks swelled as if he was trying to come up with something cutting in response. It was a futile gesture.

Damien took one step towards him and with one hand shoved Bryce into the compartment. The low heel of Bryce's shoe caught in the gap and he sprawled backwards, crashing like a deck of cards into the corner.

Then the lift doors hummed closed.

Damien watched the doors for a few seconds, as if ensuring Bryce was truly gone, before turning back to her.

She lifted her face to meet his, saw his eyes soften and warm as they swept over her face, and his gaze rocked her soul. He was fantastic. Did he have any idea of just what he'd done for her? There was no way she could have faced a scene at home tonight with Bryce pushing his way into their house. Her mother just couldn't handle that sort of stress. But Damien's actions had meant that there was no likelihood of having Bryce crashing her home and upsetting her mother. Damien had saved them both.

And it hit her then, like a blow to the gut. What

she felt now towards Damien was much more than grateful thanks. She didn't just appreciate what he'd done.

She loved him.

She loved the father of her child.

And he knew. Somehow, by whatever means, he already knew the truth about the baby. Maybe that might pave the way for a future for them all together.

She smiled up at him. It felt weak and lopsided but she couldn't stop herself from smiling with the surge of these novel and profound emotions welling up inside.

'How long have you known?' she said.

Frown lines appeared at his brow and his eyes muddied. 'Known what?'

'You know. About the b—'

All at once she realised what he'd done. That in order to get rid of Bryce the simplest way had been to turn his accusations back on him and agree that the baby was his. And it had worked. So well that even she'd been convinced he believed it.

'Oh, my God,' she said.

He grabbed her then, his hands like iron bands on her arms, wrenching her up from the chair to face him, his eyes dark and menacing and searching for answers.

'How long have I known *what* exactly?'

His fingers bit into her flesh even as she tried to form the words. 'You're hurting me.'

He let go so suddenly her knees buckled beneath her and she swayed, battling to keep her balance. His large hands caught her before she hit the ground and he swung her up until she crashed against his chest, firm and strong, the clean, masculine smell of him the last thought in her head before everything went blank.

CHAPTER EIGHT

'WHERE am I?' She came to with a start on an unfamiliar bed in equally unfamiliar surroundings. Only the city skyline, outlined through the wall of windows to her side, looked vaguely familiar.

'Relax,' Damien said, easing her shoulders back down on the soft pillow. 'You're in my penthouse apartment. I thought it would be more comfortable than the sofa in my office. Here,' he said, indicating the tray on the side table next to her, 'have something to drink. I brought juice and water—your choice.'

Her gaze skidded half-heartedly over the tray. This was his apartment? Then that meant— Her eyes swung around the room, taking in the personal effects on the dresser, the silk robe hanging on a door, and she swallowed.

His bed.

She made a wobbly move to push herself up. 'I'm sorry. I should get back to work.'

'No.' His hand on her shoulder barred her rising. 'Not until you tell me what's going on.'

She looked up at him, the underlying menace in his soft words echoed in the shadows in his eyes.

'I want to know what you meant back then.'

Still she fought it. She'd thought he'd known—it could all have been so simple.

'I want to know. You made it sound as if your pregnancy had something to do with me.'

Her eyelids fell shut on a deep breath. 'Damien,'

she said, 'please let me up. I can't explain with you standing over me.'

With a sound of impatience he twisted his body up and away from the bed. She followed by slowly swinging her legs over the edge, sitting still for a second, testing whether her legs would give way again before she too pushed herself up and away, her hands smoothing her hair as she walked to the wall of windows on the far side of the room.

'Well?' he prompted, the decibels in his voice up a notch. 'Go ahead and explain then.'

She clutched her arms around her middle, staring at the floor and trying to find words that would make her news more palatable. It would be bad enough for him to realise that he'd slept with her without the double blow that she was pregnant with his child.

But there was no easy way to say it. No way to smooth the impact of the words.

'It's true,' she said at last. 'I'm carrying your child.'

'This is ridiculous,' he said. 'We've never even had sex.'

Her head dipped in a nod. 'Obviously we have.'

'Like when? The only time we came anywhere close was at the Gold Coast and you threw me out of your room before I had hardly a chance to kiss you. Remember? So if you're pregnant from that time, someone else must be the father.' He stopped for a second, surveying her critically as if he'd just latched on to something significant.

'What did you do? Go and find good old Stu the moment I left? Is that why you were so upset with me—you had to slink back to meet him? I wondered why he wasn't too upset the next day—you'd already smoothed his wounded ego. Well, don't expect a bonus from me for what you've done just because you were away on business. It doesn't work like that.'

She unwrapped her arms from around her and felt her hands ball into fists that pounded into her thighs. 'What is your problem? Stuart wasn't upset because he didn't give a damn. He'd only asked me to go dancing. Yes, you were unnecessarily, unbearably rude that night but it wasn't exactly as if he'd asked me to marry him.

'Besides which,' she continued before he had a chance to respond. 'You really must have a pretty low opinion of me if you think I'm capable of falling into bed with any guy who crosses my path.'

'Well—' he pointedly gazed at her lower abdomen '—given your condition, you've obviously fallen into bed with somebody.'

'Maybe not,' she said, a smile emerging on her lips for the first time in their conversation. 'Who said this baby had anything to do with bed?'

'What the hell is that supposed to mean? And if you're saying it didn't happen while we were at the Gold Coast, when else have we been together long enough for this amazing conception to have taken place?'

She looked right at him, desperate to take the smug look off his face. 'The office Christmas party.'

'You weren't even there. You said—'

'*Sam* said I wasn't there. I told you my mother was ill.'

He looked at her for a moment, his face a tangle of confused emotion. 'Can't you think of anything more original than that? Are you that desperate to pin this baby on me? Maybe I should have left you to

Bryce, after all. Seems to me you two are made for each other.'

His words stung her deeply but not half as deeply as the realisation that her fears were true. He simply couldn't abide the thought of having made love to her. Damien DeLuca would never have stooped to such a thing.

Well, damn him! It was the truth. He had to believe her.

'I didn't realise it would be so confusing for you. Tell me, exactly how many women *did* you make love to in the boardroom that night?'

Something in his eyes flared. Disbelief? Panic?

'No,' he said. 'It's not possible.'

'Oh, it's more than just possible,' she said with a smile that should have hinted at much more.

'Then tell me what you were wearing.'

She allowed the corners of her mouth to kick up another notch. Still he was fighting the inevitable. 'I was dressed as Cleopatra. You were Mark Antony.'

'And that proves exactly nothing. Other people would have seen us together. How do I know what you are saying is the truth?'

She sighed, remembering the words he'd greeted her with, the words that had warmed her soul deep and fixed her in his spell. 'You said you'd been waiting two thousand years for me,' she remembered, her voice barely more than a whisper as she recalled that special moment.

'You could have overheard that.'

'True,' she acknowledged, her good feelings evaporating in the harshness of his desert-dry tone. 'So maybe I should tell you about how you locked the door behind us and lifted me on to the boardroom table, the way you released my breasts into your hands and mouth. Or maybe I should tell you how you entered me, naked but for the leather on your feet...'

Watching his face, she caught the exact moment he realised there was no escape, caught his eyes darkening, the pupils dilating as if letting in the truth at last, the slideshow of emotions—surprise, shock and outrage moving fast over his features as he digested the news.

'That was *you*?'

He sounded appalled. She'd expected nothing less but the words sliced into her all the more deeply now, knowing how she felt about him.

'Hard to believe, I know.'

Hard to believe? He'd spent how many hours trying to track down the mysterious woman who'd plagued his hard, lonely nights and filled his dreams with unrelenting frequency since the ball and here she was, right under his nose the whole time. Yet still something didn't make sense.

'But your perfume—it wasn't the same.'

For a moment she looked shocked. 'No, it wasn't. I wore my mother's perfume that night. It seemed to go better with the outfit.'

So it was her. The woman in the filmy gown, with lush red lips and a body to die for, was none other than Philly, his little brown mouse—his little not-so-brown mouse—as it turned out. And she was here now.

In his bedroom.

Serendipity.

A very happy accident indeed, he considered, congratulating himself for preferring the privacy of his apartment to the sofa in his office when she'd collapsed. There was more than a little justice in the arrangement.

He moved closer. 'I'll need proof, of course.'

Her eyes darted up to his, uncertainty flickering in their hazel lights. 'What? You mean DNA testing?'

'Eventually, yes.' He took another step closer, angling himself so that he was between the door and any escape route. She edged back against the wall of windows and he smiled to himself. There was no escape that way. 'I was thinking of something much simpler for now.'

'What do you mean?' Now she'd just about plastered herself to the glass.

He came to a stop right in front of her. 'You were wearing a mask. Even though you seem to know the details, someone could have told you.'

She moved to make a sound—a protest—but he shushed her with a finger pressed to her lips.

'I just need to be sure you are who you say you are. If I'm to believe this story of a baby, I need to know it was you that I slept with.'

He looked down at her, noticed the kick of her chin as she swallowed, enjoying the play of emotions skitter across her eyes—perplexity, fear and something else.

Anticipation?

Oh yes, without a doubt if the outline of her peaked nipples through her summer dress was any indication.

'What did you have in mind?'

He lifted a hand and she flinched. 'Relax,' he urged, his voice set to reassurance. 'You were wearing a mask. I just wondered how you looked with your eyes covered—just to be sure.'

Her eyes blinked twice and she relaxed a fraction though her breathing was still tight. It wasn't the only thing, he reflected, shifting slightly as he lifted his arm, placing his hand palm down across her eyes. Her lashes moved against his skin, soft and like the touch of a feather before they fluttered closed.

'There,' he said, his voice little more than a whisper, 'that's more like it. Now, lift your head towards me so I can see you properly.'

His hand under her chin tilted her face higher. Her breathing was shallow, her breath warm and inviting and there was no way he was going to be able to resist.

'Are you convinced now?' Her voice was tremulous and soft, her breath sweet on his face.

'Almost,' he said. 'Just one more thing.'

He dipped his head and angled his mouth over hers, brushing her lips with his. Her startled response turned into a shudder and so he deepened his kiss, parting her lips and probing further inside. When her tongue meshed with his he removed the hand over her eyes and brought it behind, holding her away from the glass and closer to him.

He sensed her arms flailing momentarily until they settled around him and her hands tightened to fists bunching up his shirt and it was her turn to pull him closer.

It was her. There was no mistake. He could stop now and be satisfied that what she said was true, that she had been the woman in the boardroom. But why should he stop?

Redundant question, he realised as his lips trailed a line down her neck. He had no intention of stopping. Not when he'd been searching for this woman ever since that night. And he hadn't been searching for her all this time to let her go again.

Her breathing was coming fast, her chest rising and falling rapidly against his and making him painfully aware of her breasts and their inaccessibility in this straight dress. His hand released her head, slid lower until it found what he was looking for. He tugged on the tab gently and slid it down to where it ended low down on her back in one silky movement. Her head jerked back, as if suddenly aware of what he was doing, but his mouth took hers again, his tongue tracing the line of her teeth, his teeth nipping at her lips while his hands slid into the gap and up under the fabric across her skin. She gasped into his mouth at the same time that her whole body moved with tremors of promise and expectation.

With his hands he slipped the dress over her shoulders, gently easing her arms down so that it could fall to the floor.

She let it go reluctantly, as if she was doing battle with herself. So be it. Whatever the outcome of her own personal dilemma, however she resolved the battles raging inside, he was intending to win the war. He crushed her to him, feeling the press of her flesh hard up against him, nothing between him and her naked form but a fine lace bra and a tiny white matching thong that left her rounded cheeks exposed to his touch. He groaned as his hands cupped them, pushing her even closer to his aching hardness.

Before she had a chance to change her mind he lifted her, her skin smooth and cool yet at the same time on fire under his hands, and swivelled her around and across to the bed.

She was certifiably insane. She must be, to let

Damien do this to her. Five minutes ago he'd been accusing her of sleeping with someone else. She should be so offended she'd never think of giving him even the time of day.

And yet there was definitely something to be said for being insane. She sank into the soft down quilt and writhed under Damien's hot mouth, currently blazing a trail towards her breasts, relishing the sensations triggered in her flesh.

Because sanity had no place here. Logic had ceased to exist. Feelings took precedence and what she was feeling now, what Damien was making her feel, was extravagant and pervasive enough to block out every other rational thought.

Except one. He wanted her. She'd expected rejection to follow the disbelief; she'd been prepared for it. No way would he have expected her to turn out to be the woman he'd made love to in the boardroom. But it hadn't happened that way. He hadn't rejected her.

He wanted her!

His mouth moved lower, fingers tracing under the edge of her bra and hot breath met her lace-covered nipple, already exquisitely sensitive with her early pregnancy, setting off spears of sensation that pierced her deep inside. Her back arched and she shuddered into his mouth.

Nothing else existed, nothing else mattered, but what he was doing to her and the way he made her feel.

Special.

Beautiful.

Loved?

No. That was what she wanted, not what he was

giving. He wasn't the kind of guy to fall in love. And right now she'd settle for feeling special. Right now she'd settle for feeling beautiful.

A noise, half purr, half groan, escaped her. And right now she'd settle for more of what his magic hot mouth was doing to her breasts—and lower…

Her fingers curled in the quilt as his hands caressed her, his tongue possessing her, circling her navel and driving her crazy with want and need as he deftly discarded her lace underwear. He touched her on her now exposed flesh and her breath caught with the intensity of the feeling. Nerve-endings she'd never known existed all but screamed their presence, their effect expanding inwards, waves of pleasure rippling to her every extremity only to come crashing back again at her core.

What force magnified mere touch to make it so bold, so all-consuming that it carried her away on its tide? Whatever it was, it was beyond comprehension, beyond dispute. Instead she let herself go with it as his tongue dipped lower, unable to fight the onslaught of heat and sensation on her skin and deeper, much deeper, inside.

She wanted more of this. She wanted more of him.

She wanted so much more…

Nothing would ease this delicious torture but having him deep inside her.

'Please…' she begged, the agony of her need rendering her powerless in his hands. And he gave something like a low growl and pulled away from her so abruptly that she felt his absence like a snapshot of grief. Her eyes fluttered open to see him looking down at her as his shoes and clothes came off, a flurry of leather and fabric until only air separated their naked skin. And then even the air was gone.

He lay down next to her, pulling her close, his smouldering eyes fixed on hers as he brushed a strand of hair from her cheek.

'You are so beautiful,' he said. 'I've dreamed of having you again ever since that night.'

And before her heart had a chance to swell he rolled her beneath him and entered her in one swift, deep movement.

And then it was his turn to cry out, something guttural and indiscernible, but which spoke of his hunger and need.

She clutched his shoulders, momentarily relishing the feeling of completion with him deep inside, pulsing with life and heat before he moved, easing back, teetering on the edge before stretching her full again.

She responded to him, meeting his rhythm, joining him in the dance as he repeated the movement, again and again, slowly, then faster, building the pace and her anticipation until he slowed again, driving her to the edge of need and desperation as her hips urged him home.

She felt his need peaking with hers and spurred him on, angling her hips to meet him as he drove himself deeper with every plunge, building her higher and higher with the magic of his rhythm until his whole body powered into hers with one final shuddering thrust. She went with him, her senses exploding in a thousand directions that started and ended at the place he now pulsed within.

For a while they lay there, bodies slick with limbs entwined as their breathing returned to something like normal and their bodies cooled, their craving and desire burned up in the fire of their passion—burned up yet far from extinguished. He shifted so his head was lying across her stomach and with his hand he traced circles over her abdomen, his light touch hypnotising her skin at the same time that it stirred her nerve endings.

'So somewhere inside here—there's a baby growing.'

His words took her by surprise. He'd hardly reacted to her news that she was pregnant to him—it certainly hadn't seemed to have had any impact—until now. Did he have no concept of what a child meant? Was the idea of family that foreign to him?

'What happened to your family?'

His hand stopped and dropped back to his side as he swung his gaze up to the ceiling.

For a while she didn't think he was going to answer, his steady breathing the only sound in the spare masculine room.

She touched her hand to his head, stroking his hair with her fingers.

'I'm sorry,' she said. 'I didn't mean to pry.'

He caught her hand in his, brought it to his mouth, and pressed her open palm against his lips with a half kiss, half sigh. 'It's okay. I don't think about it too much.'

'It must have been awful.' She knew loss. The death of her brother and his family had been bad enough. She didn't have to know the details to understand that losing his parents and possibly other members of his family too at such a young age must have been devastating.

'They had a market garden near Adelaide, where they'd settled after coming out from Italy. It was only small to start, but they built it up and when they could they did picking work as well—apples or pears—before the tomato season really kicked in. I was the youngest so I stayed home but they took my two older brothers—Santo and Jo. Before the tomato crop ripened they could make more in one day picking than the market garden could make in a week. It was my job to look after the garden.'

'How old were your brothers then?'

'Thirteen and fourteen. Santo was the image of Dad; he was so proud of him.'

'What happened?'

He made a sound, a sigh mixed with a note of despair, and she noticed his whole body tense. 'The orchard they were working on was up in the hills. They hitched a ride in the back of a pick-up truck with a bunch of others from the city. The access road was narrow, a steep dirt track with no safety rail. A car came round a bend the other way. The truck swerved to miss it but too far, too close to the edge. Once the front wheel went over there was no hope…'

Her breath caught as she imagined the horror of the accident and its impact on a young child. 'You lost everyone?'

'There were fourteen packed into the back of the truck. Only two survived. They didn't stand a chance when it rolled.'

He took a deep breath and raised a hand to rub his temple. 'I didn't know about it until the next day. It took the police that long to identify everyone.'

'You spent the night alone?'

He shrugged against her belly. 'You get used to it,' he said, his voice flat.

'That's so unfair,' she said. 'Did you have other family who could take you in?'

'No. Not in Australia and my two remaining grand-parents in Italy were too frail and I didn't want to go back. I'd grown up here. Even though my roots were Italian, I felt Australian, I belonged here. The market garden was sold—it barely covered the debts—and I ended up in foster care—' He gave a brief laugh. 'For a while, anyway. They didn't want me and I didn't need them. I worked as hard as I could at school and earned myself a scholarship and then escaped to Melbourne first chance I got.'

'So this child will be your only family,' she said, thinking aloud.

He lifted himself from the bed in one rapid move-ment and scooped up his clothes and she cursed her-self for provoking his change in mood. This was a guy who had made it in the world without family. He certainly wasn't going to be thrilled about having it thrust upon him.

'I have to get back to work. What do you plan to do?'

She laughed, low and brittle. 'I would have thought it's a bit late for planning. I'm going to have a baby. How's that for a plan?'

'You're keeping it then?'

Something congealed cold and hard in her heart.

He'd just made love to her.

She was carrying his child.

If she'd had any hopes that either one of those meant he'd consider her as something a trifle more special than plain old Philly-from-marketing, he'd just smashed those hopes to smithereens. 'I'm disap-pointed you could even ask.'

'Oh, don't feel so aggrieved. How am I expected to know what you intend to do? It's not like we really know each other.'

True, she thought, seeking the refuge of her own clothes. But that doesn't stop you wanting to make love to me. That doesn't stop me wanting you to.

And it certainly doesn't stop me loving you.

'So what do you expect from me?'

She looked up at him, her hazel eyes focused acutely on his, hoping they conveyed the sense of cold he'd just doused her with. Much as it would have been easier never to have let Damien know that he was the father, she'd done the right thing. He now knew about the baby. Her responsibility to him ended right there. If he wasn't prepared to have anything to do with this child, then she'd be more than happy to assume sole responsibility. It would sure save any complications.

'What do I expect from you? Absolutely nothing.'

His face starkly displayed his disbelief. But then, why would he believe her? No doubt he'd be expecting her to take full advantage of the benefits of a rich father for her child.

'It's true,' she said. 'I don't want anything from you.'

'You think you can do this all by yourself?'

'Of course I can.' *If I have to.* 'It's what I want.' *If that's what it takes.*

'What about what I want?'

'It's obvious you don't want to be involved. You've made that perfectly clear by even assuming I could do anything other than keep this child. You didn't ask for this to happen. You didn't ask for a child.'

'And you did?'

Her eyes dropped to the floor. He'd never understand if she told him. He'd never understand how much this baby meant, how much it would mean to her mother and how she'd dreamed so fervently of having a child. But those reasons had nothing to do with him. He didn't need to know.

'Of course it was a shock,' she said. 'But now that I've accepted it I'm going to do everything I can to make this child's life worthwhile. This baby's never going to feel like it's not wanted or that its life is the result of a mistake. I'm going to make it a home.'

'Very noble sentiments. And just how do you plan on doing all this by yourself?'

'I'll manage.'

'You'll manage,' he echoed hollowly, his voice dry and flat. 'A single mother, either unable to work or having to put the child into care all day and scraping by on a pittance if you can work. Is that how you intend to manage?'

She knew it wasn't going to be easy—she'd never thought that. But hearing him put it like that— She swallowed, attempting to bury her doubts and regain the confidence she'd felt when she'd worked out that this was what she should do. 'Lots of women do. They get by.'

'Not with my child they don't!'

The vehemence of his words took her by surprise. Was this really the man with the reputation of a confirmed bachelor and dedicated non-family man?

'Then what are you suggesting? Some sort of financial support for the child?'

'Not just that,' he said as he looped his tie deftly into the perfect knot. 'Something much more appro-

priate for all of us. An arrangement that will mean
you don't have to worry about balancing work with
child-care. Something that will ensure your and the
child's security for life.'

Her breath caught as a tingle of sensation bubbled
inside. No, it wasn't possible. Surely he wasn't about
to suggest marriage? But what else could offer the
security the child needed, the solid foundation for a
future life?

Maybe she'd underestimated him. Marriage didn't
sound like something the commitment-averse Damien
would suggest to anyone, least of all to her. Did the
existence of a baby make so much difference, that
now she was worthy of consideration as his bride,
now she was considered marriage material?

Marriage.

Marriage to Damien.

How would it feel to be Damien's wife? To wake
up alongside him every day, to feel his strong body
holding her safe at night, to make a family with him.

To have his child and to have him too—dreams
were made of lesser stuff.

So he didn't love her. She knew that. But they
could still make it work. She loved him and she'd
make it work if it meant pretending to be Cleopatra
every night to do it. She'd do whatever it took.

It would be worth it.

She waited, almost too scared to breathe, unable to
speak and ask what he could possibly mean. After
what seemed an age he returned from the bathroom,
his hair restored to its usual executive state, the tracks
of her fingernails obliterated.

'I have a property, out of the city about one hundred kilometres or so. I can't get out there as much

as I'd like but the house is in good condition and there's a full-time housekeeper and manager.

'It'll be a perfect place for you to bring the child up,' he continued. 'I'll pay all the household expenses and give you an allowance as well so you don't have to worry about working.'

A freezing dump of despair oozed over her and it was seconds before she could convince her jaw to thaw enough to let her speak.

'You'd set me up in a house of yours?'

He shrugged. 'It's the best option for both of us. I'll visit on weekends when I can get away.'

'And what of my mother? Who would look after her? No, Damien. There's no way.'

'She can come too. There's plenty of room. You can all be together.'

'Thanks so much for your kind offer, but I'm sorry, I'm not actually in the market for a new home. Maybe some other time…'

She pushed past him, trying to reach the bathroom and find a place where she could breathe again, a place where she could think, but he grabbed her arm, wheeling her around.

'Listen to me. I'm offering this child a home, security. I'll arrange the best doctors for your mother, the best paediatricians for the baby. The child will have everything it needs.' His fingers tightened on her arm. 'What are you waiting for—a better offer?'

'Lovely to know you're so concerned about this child. And what will my role be in this arrangement?'

'You'll bring up the child. I take it that's what you expect to do? And you won't have to do housework or the cooking and cleaning or worry about a day job. I'll even get private nursing for your mother, and on top of everything I'll pay you for the privilege. So maybe you could try to be a bit more grateful.'

'*Grateful!* And let me guess—will I also be expected to share your bed whenever you feel the urge? Is that how you expect me to show how grateful I am? Am I expected to extend my gratitude to you on my back?'

She wrenched her arm but his grip merely tightened, locked on, his fingers like steel manacles. She suppressed a gasp as his fingers bit into her flesh. He might be stronger than she was, but still she wasn't going to give him the satisfaction of knowing that he was hurting her.

He drew her closer, so close that she could see the white-hot fury in his eyes, feel his heated breath on her cheek. One side of his lips kicked up in a smile that went no further. 'You didn't seem to have a problem with being flat on your back ten minutes ago. Or have you forgotten already how good I made you feel, how you bucked under me until I blew your world apart?'

Her pulse hammered, her temple throbbed, as her heart cranked up the pressure through her veins as his dark eyes locked on hers. She could never forget how he made her feel, not in this life.

'Have you forgotten already how you begged me to take you?' His free hand cupped her breast. Her shocked intake of breath was fast and tremulous as he massaged the tender flesh, her nipple firming and reaching out into his palm.

He closed the gap between them, pushing himself against her. She felt his arousal with shock and awe, excitement building in her own deep places.

'Are you seriously telling me you wouldn't like to make love with me again?'

His hand left her breast and dipped down her back, pressing her into his hardness. 'Are you seriously trying to tell me you don't want me again?'

His words were seductive, hypnotising her, a mantra for her soul. His touch was persuasive, compulsive, like a mantra for her body.

He dropped a hand into her still open zipper, slipping his hand down until his warm fingers cupped the flesh of one cheek, squeezing, massaging, his fingers exploring more...

'There's no denying it, you realise that. You want me just as much as I want you.'

'Damien,' she half-pleaded, sensation blotting out rational thought once more, nerve-endings screaming for release. It was true. She could no more deny wanting him than she could deny the sun a place in the sky. But that didn't mean he could buy her like just one more part of his business.

'See,' he said, a tone of victory injected into his voice. 'There's no way you can deny me. Not now.'

'Damien,' she said, stronger this time, his arrogance fuelling her determination to fight back. 'I won't be your mistress.'

'You don't mean that,' he said. 'Let me show you what you really want.' His mouth dipped lower as if intending to claim hers but it never made its mark. Summoning strength she didn't know she possessed, she pushed and twisted at the same time, swivelling out of his arms and swaying across the room until dozens of cubic metres of super-charged air swirled between them.

'Believe me, Damien. I won't be your mistress. I

won't be *anyone's* mistress. Have you no idea what an insult that is?'

'Then what were you expecting? Marriage? Is that what you were hoping for? A white picket fence and a fairy-tale ending?'

She schooled her face blank, her chest heaving, not trusting her voice to hold steady if she uttered a word. Of course it sounded ridiculous when he put it like that. But what was wrong with wanting things to be right, wanting to bring up a child in a proper family? What was wrong with hoping love might have something to do with it?

But there was no way she'd tell Damien that.

'Don't be ridiculous,' she said, only when she was sure her voice wouldn't betray her. 'I told you, I don't want anything from you.'

Still, his eyes narrowed, focusing on something in her face. 'Ah, but that's what you were hoping for, wasn't it?'

His words cut uncomfortably close to the truth. Why had she had to go and fall in love with him? It had been so much easier in the beginning, before she'd seen beyond the arrogant businessman behind whom Damien existed, before she'd felt his lovemaking and experienced the sheer magic of his touch.

Until then she'd been happy to think about a life with her child—Damien didn't even have to figure. But she did love him. And now she couldn't imagine life with his child without him.

Her chin kicked up. 'You must really fancy yourself. I told you and I mean it. I don't want anything from you.'

He watched her for a few seconds more, cold emotion drizzling down over them. 'So be it. Because I don't do family. It's not going to happen.'

He walked to the slatted timber bifold doors separating the bedroom from the rest of the apartment. 'I'm going back to work. Let yourself out when you're ready.'

'I'll be down shortly,' she said, knowing it would take her a good ten minutes to get herself back together enough to appear in public.

'Don't bother,' he said. 'Go home.'

And then he was gone.

CHAPTER NINE

'How is she?' asked Enid on his return.

'Gone home,' he snapped back, 'and if she's got any sense, she'll stay there.'

Enid's eyes narrowed speculatively, her lips tight and puckered. 'I see.'

'You do? I sure wish the hell I did. Hold my calls, Enid. Tell everyone I'm in conference.'

'As you wish,' she said as he entered his office. He closed the door behind him but for once ignored the expansive desk to his right. Instead he strode to the wall of glass, his window to the outside world, and gazed out across the city, looking for answers amongst the columns of office towers, the low-rise buildings and homes at the city's fringe and the warehouses of the harbour near the port. The sea lay lifeless in the distance, flat and dull. He empathised. It matched his mood perfectly.

It had been one hell of a day. To finally find the woman who'd been haunting his thoughts and dreams for so long only to discover it had been Philly all along. What was more, to learn she was pregnant with his child.

He was going to be a father.

The concept was as exciting as it was terrifying. Yet he didn't want a child; he'd never wanted one. He'd survived without the whole family thing for this long. He didn't need it.

So why did some small part of him insist on feeling

proud? He'd spent his life avoiding such possibilities with a vengeance. So why didn't he break out in a cold sweat as he'd expect? Why did he feel such a sense of exhilaration at the idea?

He was going to be a father.

He was going to have a child.

And, no matter what Philly said, he would make sure that child was properly taken care of.

What was her problem, anyway? He'd just offered her a house, a housekeeper, nursing care for her mother and an income. She wouldn't have to lift a finger. It was a great deal.

So why wouldn't she accept? What did she want? He'd made her a reasonable offer. More than reasonable. And she'd turned him down flat.

He sighed deeply, his forehead and hands pressed against the glass as he looked down to the street below. It was a long way down. He'd been down there, at rock bottom and lower, not even within cooee of a rung to begin the long, lonely climb up the ladder.

And he'd made it. All the way to the top on his own. No one to help him, no one to turn to for support but a drunken foster mother who had drunk his foster money blind and the faded memory of a family tragedy that had taught him never to get close to anyone.

He lashed out with his foot, slamming his shoe into the reinforced glass and making the entire window shudder before he spun around and tracked a course round his desk.

What the hell was wrong with him? He hadn't thought so much about his family for years and yet today, in the feel-good hum of some of the best sex he'd had since their encounter in the boardroom—the *only* sex he'd had since that encounter in the boardroom—the mere suggestion of a honeyed voice had dredged it all up.

He paced the carpet, trying not to ignore the pictures that were surfacing in his mind's eye, the pictures like dusty film clips he'd been avoiding for years. His father, tall and straight, strong featured, with hair swept back much like his own, but greying already at the temples, the white shirt and dark trousers, his standard uniform; even when picking fruit or working in the garden he had always liked to look his best.

His brothers, loud and broad-shouldered like their father and always wrestling in the yard outside when they should have been doing homework.

And his mother, dark and handsome, with eyes that had sparkled with love and pride, scolding her two eldest sons only to toss her thick, dark hair and leave them, laughing as she'd turned back to her cooking.

He sucked in a jagged breath and closed his eyes but the pictures became even sharper and more distinct.

Unrelated snippets of memories exploded into his mind like the coloured contents of a party popper.

These were real people he was remembering, not some cardboard cut-outs that could be neatly filed away in a corner of his mind, buried deeper than the four wooden caskets that had lain side by side in the old church.

They'd been his family and now they were gone. And he'd done his best to leave them behind, moving cities, moving states. Burying them in his mind.

He shivered.

Suddenly he had to get out of there. Had to go somewhere—*anywhere*. He pulled open the door in time to see Philly placing some papers on Enid's desk. She jerked around guiltily at his appearance, her face pale but her eyes challenging. Then she frowned and her features softened into something closer to concern. She took a step towards him.

'Are you okay?' she asked.

'What are you doing here?' he demanded. 'I told you to go home.'

She stopped dead, her back stiffening. 'I've just had two weeks leave. I have work to catch up on.'

'You're not fit for work.'

'I'm pregnant,' she said, forcing herself taller as if that would convince him. 'I'm not ill.'

'What do you call what happened this morning then?'

Her chin kicked up even as she coloured.

'I think most people refer to it as sex.'

'Not that,' he snarled. 'When you fainted.'

'I'm over it. That won't happen again.'

'We'll see.' He looked around, settling his gaze on Enid's empty chair before striding to the lift. 'Tell Enid I'm going out.'

'When will you be back?'

'I don't know,' he said as he allowed himself to be swallowed up by the hungry cavern of the lift.

'I don't know.'

CHAPTER TEN

HE DIDN'T know where he was heading.

Anywhere.

Nowhere.

It didn't matter. He drove aimlessly with no sense of direction and less sense of time until something drew him towards the coast. It was sunny, the day was fine, the top of his black BMW convertible was down and his passing drew envious looks from the men in cars around him, wishful glances from the women.

Normally he'd get a buzz out of the experience, a fillip to his ego, the successful businessman out enjoying the spoils of his success.

Success.

How did you measure that? In dollars and cents, in bricks and buildings, corporate takeovers and fast cars? Sure, on that score he was as successful as they came, no question.

Or was success measured in more human terms—in connections built between people, in relationships, *in families*?

The human factor.

On that score, so far all he'd been successful at was avoiding that very thing. But now he was going to be a father and the one thing he'd evaded for so long was happening.

A father. Why did that change things so much?

Why should that suddenly make his business success ring so hollow?

Finally he left the highway and crossed the train lines before pulling alongside the kerb, opposite a battered brick veneer house in a post-war building boom suburb.

What was he doing here? He'd never been here before, he'd just snatched a glimpse of the address in some papers on Enid's desk one day. Amazing he'd even remembered it.

He studied the house. It had seen better days by the look of the shabby brickwork, the flaking window-frames and the tired garden, its leggy native plants wafting listlessly in the warm breeze. Once he was out of the car he could just smell the sea, the tang of seaweed and salt in the air, though the beach was nothing more than a dull promise across the train tracks and beyond the strip of kiosks and mid-rate hotels lining the highway.

He'd never asked her about her home. He'd never asked her how her mother was. It had never occurred to him. But now it seemed important. He wanted to know more about her, about the woman who was to be his child's mother, about her family.

He knocked on the door. And waited.

The clang of the crossing barriers started up, loud and insistent, as a train surged along the track, all electric whine and squealing metal before gradually the noise died down and quiet resumed. He thought about leaving but had no idea where he'd go. The train was probably already at the next station when he finally heard a sound inside the house, spotted a blurred shape moving through the panel of misted glass.

The door edged open, a security chain clamping in place. Through the gap he could see her wary gaze, in dark-ringed eyes that looked almost too big in her sunken face.

'Mrs Summers?'

'Yes,' came her voice, brittle and shaky and obviously unused to visitors during the day.

'My name is Damien DeLuca. Philly works—'

'Oh, my,' she said, panic swamping her eyes as she unlatched the door and shoved it open. 'Is she all right? Has something happened to her?'

He held up his hands. 'No, no. She's fine. Really.' He watched the panic recede and cursed himself for his stupidity. 'I didn't mean to alarm you. I was—just passing. I thought I'd drop in—for a chat.'

One of her hands went to the wispy dull fuzz of her hair, the other clutched a walking stick in a white knuckled grip.

Cancer. She had cancer and she'd lost her hair from the chemotherapy. She was tiny, a tinier version of Philly, and paper-thin under the buttoned up house-coat.

He bristled in irritation. Why hadn't Philly told him? He'd had no idea. How on earth was she managing a full-time job and caring for her mother?

'Well,' she said in a voice which was frail, yet years younger than she looked. 'I'm not really dressed for visitors, but it's lovely to meet you. And please call me Daphne. You know, I've heard such a lot about you.'

'You have?'

'Of course. You're a very talented young man by the sounds of it. Philadelphia's told me how you like to rule the roost. Would you like a cup of tea?'

He somehow managed to nod while digesting that brief and unexpected character sketch. 'Thank you.'

She shuffled her way into the small kitchen and made for the kettle. 'I'm sorry to take so long to answer the door. I'm not as fast as I used to be.'

He looked at her, struggling with the walking stick to move around, wincing with the effort every few steps and trying unsuccessfully to mask the pain.

'Please,' he said, sidestepping her. 'I'm the one interrupting you; let me get it. Why don't you sit down?'

She looked up at him, surprised, as if his offer of help was the last thing she'd expected—just what had Philly told her?—before a smile illuminated her gaunt face. 'Thank you. I could do with a sit down even though that seems to be all I do these days.' She showed him where everything was and with a sigh eased herself into an armchair while he made the tea.

'I must thank you for sending Marjorie while Philadelphia was away,' she said when Damien placed their tea on the table and sat down opposite. 'She was a wonderful companion.'

For a moment he scrabbled to get his head around who she was talking about. Then he realised. The trip to the Gold Coast—the nurse he'd had Enid organise. 'It was no trouble,' he said, casting his mind over the unwashed breakfast dishes in the sink, the picked over lunch tray waiting on the bench. It was clear Daphne could do with a little help every day.

'How do you manage here, by yourself, during the day?'

'Oh, we get by. Philadelphia gets me organised in the mornings and fixes me a tray for lunch.' She sipped at her tea. 'If I have a good day I try to start dinner to help her when she comes home from work, though sometimes it doesn't quite work that way.'

He nodded blankly, his mind working overtime. What the hell was Philly thinking? This was no way to live, leaving her mother alone all day out here in the suburbs, while she worked at least twenty kilometres away in the city. And yet she'd turned down his offer of a house with carers and laid on help, *and* she'd turned it down flat. Did she think she was managing here any better than he could provide for them? If so, she was kidding herself.

Would her mother have found his offer so unattractive? Casting an eye around the simply decorated room, neat and tidy but long overdue for repainting and renovation at the very least, he doubted it.

But this wasn't just about Philly and her mother now. If she thought for a moment he would let her bring up his child in such circumstances, then she could think again.

'You must find things very difficult.'

'It's harder for Philadelphia. She's my only child now.' She looked up, the pain of loss in her eyes unmistakable. 'Did you know about…?'

He nodded. 'Yes, I heard.' He could almost feel her loss reach out to encompass him, a thick, tangible thing. Or was it simply that his own loss was now so close to the surface that he could just about taste it?

Philly had done that. Had brought these feelings to the surface, feelings that were better off left to moulder deep down below.

He swallowed, as if that would bury these unwanted feelings deeper again. He knew loss just as surely as did the wasted woman sitting opposite him. *Loss.* Such a tiny word yet it was so big—larger and more encompassing than anything anyone could ever warn you about. And if you couldn't deal with it, tuck it away and bury it in the back of your mind, it could take over your life.

So he'd buried it. Deep down inside him, concealing the site under a ton of concrete will. Until today. He groaned inwardly.

Oh, hell, yes, he knew loss.

'That must have been terrible for you,' he said.

Her eyes misted, a silent affirmation. 'And of course that means that Philadelphia has to do it all, I'm afraid. She's stuck with me and she knows I want to stay at home as long as possible.'

'As long as possible?'

She put her cup down and sighed. 'I will have to move into a hospice in a few months the doctors say—there's nothing else for it. Philadelphia won't be able to look after me soon and I can't expect her to. So if you're worried about me getting in the way of her work…? I imagine that's why you're here?'

She was dying. It should have been clear from the moment she opened the door—her bird-like frame, her gaunt features and pained walk. It should have been clear. But then he'd had plenty of experience in ignoring death, shoving it aside in his quest to reach the top.

She was dying and she thought he was here to find out whether Philly would still make a good employee.

'No,' he said, bursting out of the chair. 'No, that's not why I'm here.'

He paced around the small room, trying to banish the nervous tension invading his senses. But why *was* he here? What did he hope to achieve? Certainly something more than this sense of hopelessness and despair, this struggle for an answer to questions he couldn't even frame—something that would answer this desperate need he couldn't even put words to.

He stopped beside a display of photographs assembled along the mantle. The history of a family, laid out before his eyes. A wedding photograph, fading with age, showing a young Daphne and her late husband on their wedding day, smiling for the camera, happy and hopeful for the future. A photograph of the young family with two children, a boy—just a toddler—and his older sister, maybe six or seven years old, with pigtails and wearing a frilly dress.

Philly.

Just a skinny kid then, but there was no mistaking her eyes and that chin, defiant and serious even back then.

And now she was a woman. Every part a woman, as this morning's heated passion had attested. What drove her then, to deny him? Three times she'd evaded his reach. Three times she'd slipped away from him. The Christmas party when she'd stolen away, that night at the Gold Coast when she'd pushed him from her room, and today, when he'd all but offered her luxury on a platter. Still she seemed to want no part of him.

But he would have her. He'd never failed at anything in his life. Anything he'd wanted he'd strived for and achieved. Philly would be no exception.

He dragged his eyes away to the graduation photographs, the two children all grown up and about to set the world aflame. Another wedding photograph, more recent, no doubt Monty with his new bride, smiling into each other's eyes, totally oblivious to the camera. And the last one, another young family, a tiny baby cradled in its proud parents' arms.

He swallowed as he continued to stare, feeling swamped by the history, the tragedy, but most of all by the sheer force of emotion contained in the photographs so lovingly arranged on the mantle. Those most wonderful moments in a family's history recorded—disparate images of a particular moment of time—together making up a snapshot of a family's history, a pictorial chronology.

For some reason the picture of the baby drew him, its doll-like quality, the sprinkling of downy hair on its head and its surprisingly long fingers poking out from beneath its blanket as it slept.

He didn't know the first thing about babies. He'd never wanted to know. But now there was this overwhelming sense of fascination. A door had been opened to him and there was a whole new world to explore. Philly had opened that door.

'That's little Thomas,' Daphne said, her voice soft and heavy with sorrow. 'He would have turned two just last week. I can't help but think what he'd be up to now if he were still alive. No doubt toddling about everywhere, getting into everything.'

He looked over his shoulder. She was so small and weak, her sadness so much a part of her. 'You must miss them very much.'

Her nod was no more than a tilt of her head, even her gaze still fixed on the floor in front of her. 'I do, but then there's something so special about babies,' she said, as he turned back to the photograph. 'I think that's almost what I miss most—the wonder of new life, the hope for the future. It's too late for me to experience that again now.'

She sighed and reached for a handkerchief to blot the dampness from her eyes. 'Oh, just listen to me,' she croaked, almost to herself, 'rambling on like a silly old woman.'

He put the photograph down and turned, barely noticing her words as what she'd said earlier slowly permeated his consciousness.

She didn't know.

Philly hadn't told her.

Why on earth wouldn't she tell her own mother about the baby? Couldn't she see how much it would mean to her?

He looked back at the mantle, mentally seeing one more photograph—a beaming Philly holding a tiny child—another chance at life and a future.

Didn't Philly want her mother to see that photograph already? Or was she more worried about the absence of another? His eyes flicked over the wedding photographs. He could almost see the space where Philly's wedding photo would slot in alongside her brother's. Was the prospect of an illegitimate child the reason why Philly was holding off sharing the news with her mother?

Was she trying to save her mother hurt by not telling her the truth?

Something shifted inside him, sliding away to reveal a solution which was on the one hand so unexpected, yet at the same time so logical. He could help. He *wanted* to help. And he would have Philly in the bargain.

'Maybe all hope isn't gone,' he said, taking Daphne's hand in his own before sitting down. 'Maybe there's still a chance for something good, something that could give us all hope.'

She peered up at him, her dark-ringed eyes curious and hopeful at the same time. 'Whatever do you mean? Why *are* you here, Mr DeLuca?'

'I have something to tell you,' he said, struck by the fragility of her bird-like hand, her thin bones covered by barely more than a paper-thin cover of dry skin. He covered her hand with his other as if to keep her warm. 'Actually, I have something to ask of you.'

He paused, momentarily wondering if he was doing the right thing, but one look into her eyes told him that for the first time in what seemed like for ever he was doing something that mattered, something that had a beneficial effect beyond just the bottom line. And yet it would still get him what he wanted.

He took a deep breath before he continued.

'Would you give me the honour of allowing me to marry your daughter?'

CHAPTER ELEVEN

THERE. He'd said it. And it didn't feel so bad. In fact, taking in her sudden gasp of delight, the following smile which lit up the older woman's face, it felt pretty damned good.

It was the most logical solution. Philly obviously couldn't cope here, with a sick mother, a full-time job and a baby coming. And marriage would mean the baby would carry his name while Philly would bear none of the stigma attached to being a single mother.

It solved everything. Sure, he'd never intended getting married; in fact, he'd done all he could to avoid it. And he'd spent most of his lifetime alone—it wasn't as if he needed anyone—but if it meant that his child would be brought up the way he wanted, then maybe it would be worth sacrificing his independence just this once.

Because he'd get to spend his nights with Philly. That would at least be some compensation. He would have settled for mistress, but he'd marry her if that was what it took.

A key grated in the front door lock and he glanced at his watch, surprised at the late hour and realising just how much time he'd spent aimlessly driving around today.

'I'm home,' came Philly's voice from the small entrance hall. She sounded tired. She should have come home when he'd told her. Except he wouldn't have been here now if she had.

He rose to his feet and swung around alongside Daphne, his hand resting on the back of her chair.

'What are you doing here?' Philly felt the hair on the back of her neck stand up as she took in the cameo, her mother and Damien together, empty tea cups on the table where they'd sat opposite each other, much too cosily.

She should have known something was up when she'd spotted the sleek black coupé across the road. A car like that in this street was as unlikely as Damien stopping by for a cup of tea. And yet he was here...

'What's going on?'

'Sweetheart,' her mother said, battling her way to her feet with Damien's help by way of his hand under her elbow. 'Congratulations. I had no idea.' Her mother pulled her close, so close she could feel her wasted ribcage pressing into her through the thin cotton housecoat.

She glared at Damien over her mother's shoulder. 'You told her?' she said.

'Of course he told me,' said her mother, resting both her hands on Philly's shoulders. 'How else could he ask for my permission? Oh, you've made me so happy, I can't quite believe it. How soon do you plan to be married?'

'*Married?*'

She blinked as her insides lurched crazily. She'd imagined he'd spilt the beans about the pregnancy, but this... This wasn't happening. This didn't make sense. She opened her mouth, about to deny it, about to say there'd been some kind of mistake, when her eyes jagged with Damien's and the denial she expected to find echoed within his was nowhere to be seen. Instead, their dark intense depths seemed aflame with victory even as they threw out a challenge.

'Oh, married,' she said, wanting to sound as rational as possible for her mother's sake while her mind reeled with insane possibilities. 'Well, Damien and I have to talk about that. Just like we have a lot of other issues to resolve. *Don't we, Damien?*'

He smiled in response, one eyebrow arched, and not looking half as uncomfortable as she would have preferred him to. What was he up to?

Her mother broke the impasse. 'Well, this is wonderful news but I'm afraid I need to lie down for a little while now before dinner. All this excitement has worn me out. But I'm sure you two have plenty to catch up on. So if you'll excuse me, I'll just have a nap.'

'Of course,' said Philly, kissing her mother on the cheek. 'I'll see you get comfortable. We can have a late dinner tonight.'

Daphne turned to Damien, who dropped a kiss on her cheek likewise. 'Oh,' she said in response, 'if I were twenty years younger, I think I'd fancy giving you a run for your money myself.'

'If you were twenty years younger, I'd be taking you up on that.'

Her mother laughed like she hadn't heard for ages and Philly was half tempted to enjoy the sound. It was just so good to hear her mother laughing, let alone flirting. But she knew how fragile her mother was. How devastating it would be for her to realise this was all just some game Damien was playing.

Why was he doing this? What on earth was he trying to prove? She wouldn't see her mother hurt for anything or anyone. And this bizarre idea about marriage wasn't going to help anyone. Damien had had his chance earlier today and he'd made it more than clear then that he simply wasn't interested. So what was he doing here, putting thoughts of weddings and goodness knew what else into her mother's head?

Had he really not said a word yet about her pregnancy as she'd first feared? It was far too early to tell her just yet. What the hell was he playing at?

She saw her mother settled on her day bed and returned to the living room, white-hot fury building within her with every step.

Damien was waiting for her, still standing, the look on his face like a cat that had just caught a mouse. Well, this mouse was about to fight back.

'Welcome home,' he drawled, one side of his mouth curving up mockingly. 'Hard day at the office?'

'Don't "welcome home" me. We need to talk,' she said, her voice a low snarl.

'Sure,' he said easily with a shrug, as if he hadn't the least idea what she would want to talk about. 'Shoot.'

'Not here. Outside.' She didn't want any chance of her mother overhearing this conversation. She stalked through the kitchen to the rear entrance, leading the way to the small timber deck without looking back. But she knew he was there. She could feel his smug expression laughing into her back as he shadowed her out the door. She'd wipe that smug look off his face if it killed her.

She turned and somehow the deck had shrunk. The small outdoor table and chairs still took up the same space but Damien consumed the rest as he leaned his length over, propping his arms on the railing and looking out over the sun-dried back lawn and the fringe of shrubs lining the fence.

How dared he look so relaxed and at peace with the world? How dared he turn her life upside-down with a click of his fingers? And how dared he fool with the emotions of a frail, sick woman?

The fury inside her only mounted as he continued to gaze out, ignoring her completely. She crossed her arms over her chest but the action only seemed to magnify the crazy thumping of her heart.

'What are you doing here?'

He turned slowly, almost lazily, towards her, as if her question and tone were no more than the buzzing of an annoying insect somewhere nearby.

'That doesn't sound like the kind of greeting I'd expect from the woman I've just become betrothed to.'

'I never said I was going to marry you. What the hell is this all about—some kind of warped payback because I said no to your earlier demands?'

'You're having my baby, aren't you?'

'And what's that got to do with it?'

'That's got everything to do with it.'

'I thought you said you didn't do family.'

'I don't. Normally. But you can't bring up my baby here and you wouldn't come as my mistress. I had no choice. Now you have no choice.'

She let his slur on her house and what she could provide for a child slide away. She couldn't tackle everything at once. 'Did you tell my mother about the baby?'

His hands left the railing as he turned fully to face her. 'No, but I was left to wonder why you wouldn't. So now you don't have to worry about having an illegitimate child. Now your child will have a name and your baby will have a father. You could thank me for taking care of your problem.'

'*Thank you? My problem?* Tell me, where does your particular brand of arrogance come from? Did you make it yourself or did you take it over, like just another one of your corporate acquisitions?'

It was his turn to bristle, she noted with considerable satisfaction as he shifted his stance. 'Do you seriously think I haven't told my mother yet because I'm worried that she'll be devastated about me being an unmarried mother?'

'What else? You don't seem to realise how much a baby would mean to your mother. How could you not tell her such news?'

'Don't you think I know what my own mother needs? You're the last person who needs to tell me how much she would love to see another grandchild.'

'So now it's not an issue. Now you have nothing to be ashamed of.'

'I *never* had anything to be ashamed of. For your information, I haven't told my mother yet because I'm little more than six weeks' pregnant. Do you understand that?'

'You mean,' he interrupted, his face a tight frown, 'there's a chance you could be wrong?'

'No. The pregnancy has been confirmed. But that doesn't mean things can't still happen. What if I lose the baby?'

'Is that likely?'

'Not likely. But not impossible either. This is still very early days in the pregnancy. The last thing I need is for my mother to get her hopes up and then have them dashed once more. That's why I haven't told her yet—not because of some stupid idea that she won't be happy unless I have someone's ring on my finger.'

His silence lasted for barely a second and then he shrugged. 'It's of no consequence. We're getting married anyway—it's all decided. You can hardly let your mother down now.'

'And if something happens to the baby?'

'We'll have another.'

She shook her head. 'Damien, you're not listening to me. I never said I'd marry you.'

'You don't want marriage? You surprise me. That seemed to be exactly what you wanted this morning. You weren't satisfied with just my house, my servants, my income. It was clear to me you wanted more.'

'You can't just waltz in here and take over this house and this family like it's one of your business deals. Those kind of tactics might work in the boardroom, but they certainly don't wash here.'

Immediately she'd mentioned it she wished she could take it back. There was no way she could think about boardrooms without thinking of that night, of the night that had started it all, and with the memories came the heat, heat that was all the more raw after their lovemaking of today. She didn't need to remember such things now, *especially not now*, when she was trying to put distance between them, when she was trying to make him see sense.

Her eyes sought his. *Damn.* They narrowed, a predatory gleam infusing them, and she saw that he'd made the connection. With two quick steps he'd forced her backwards until his arms dropped either side of her and she was trapped.

'I'm not the only one around here who engages in boardroom tactics—or have you forgotten that first little episode?'

She shook her head as she backed up hard against the railing, fighting the sheer magnetism of his body, the pull of his body increasing with his proximity. 'No. But it's not relevant. You can't just make people do what you want. You can't just decide for them their future without a thought for their own needs and desires. You can't—'

Her words were cut off as his arms crushed her to him and his mouth found her throat, sending bold heat suffusing her veins, washing through her on a torrid tide that threatened to blow her resolve, if not her sanity.

His head forced hers back, leaving her neck and throat exposed to his mouth, his lips and tongue working together immediately finding all of those special places—that spot on her neck just below her ear lobe, the line where her skin disappeared under the neckline of her dress. All of her skin, anywhere his mouth touched, came alive and it was impossible to stop her body responding to his assault.

'You see…' His head lifted just a fraction so his lips skidded over her skin, a dance of breathy heat and liquid movement. 'See how much you want me,' he said. 'I could take you here, on the deck, and you would be powerless to stop me.'

She tried to breathe, to clear her mind. Yes, she wanted him. No matter how much she wished she could refute his claims her body would not be denied. Her heart would not be denied. She wanted him body and soul. But that still didn't make what he was doing right. It was one thing for her to give herself freely. It was another for him to take it.

'But that's the way you always operate, Damien. You take what you want.'

'You don't fool me. You want this too.'

'So why not take me then? Take me now, right here, while my mother sleeps inside. And what exactly will that prove? Do you for one moment imagine I will be so blown away by your love-making that I will be desperate enough to rush down the aisle for more?'

The change in his breathing told her that her words had hit their mark. His head twisted to rest on her shoulder as his arms relaxed their grip. He surged away towards the house without looking at her, one hand on his hip, the other sweeping back through his hair all the way down to his neck.

She was driving him crazy. He must be crazy, to want to attack her on her own back step, her mother sleeping inside the house.

But he wanted her—so much. Why did she continue to frustrate him? She'd fled from him that first night, hidden her identity and kept it concealed. And she still made out she was an innocent in all this when she'd held all the cards right from the beginning.

'You seem to take a great deal of satisfaction in pointing out my failings, but do you think your own behaviour is beyond reproach?' She looked up at him, startled, as if not expecting him to go on the attack so soon.

'What do you mean?'

'You're the one who ran away the night of the masquerade ball. You're the one who kept your identity a secret. If you hadn't told me today about the baby—' He stopped, reeling back the hours to that time.

She hadn't told him.

He'd intervened in her dispute with that loser, Bryce, and Bryce hadn't been the only one who'd believed him. In her fragile state she'd thought he was telling the truth. She'd thought he really did know the baby was his.

He looked up at her, his eyes open for what seemed the first time as the layers of her deceit peeled away.

'You weren't going to tell me, were you.'

It wasn't a question, it was an accusation. 'You were never going to tell me.'

'No, Damien, that's not true.'

'You were going to keep this baby a secret. You never intended to let me in on it. If I hadn't come to your rescue and you hadn't taken me seriously, I never would have known.'

'No! I was going to tell you today.'

'But you didn't.'

'I didn't have a chance. I was about to tell you, in your office, but Bryce—'

'Bryce nothing. I don't believe you. You've hidden the truth from me all along. Why should today be any different?'

'Because it's the truth.'

'No. You were going to keep it your secret. Another little secret. Like making love to me that night. That was your secret. You didn't want me to know who you were—that's what that mask was all about—why you wouldn't take it off. You never wanted me to find out.'

'Damien, listen to me—'

'Why should I listen to you? You've hidden the

truth all along. You hid your face that night so I wouldn't know who you were. Then you let me believe you were never at that Christmas party. Why would you do that and then suddenly decide to tell me you're pregnant and it's my baby?'

'Because it is your baby. You have a right to know.'

'You care about my rights?' he scoffed. 'I very much doubt that. But this isn't about rights. I believe you never had any intention of admitting you were in that boardroom let alone advising me that I was the father of this baby. If it hadn't been for that blunder you made when I threw Bryce out, you would never have told me.'

'Damien, that's simply not true.'

'Isn't it? You can honestly say you never once considered hiding the truth about this baby from me? You never once considered the possibility of bringing this child up on your own?'

Her eyes slid sideways before they slowly meandered their way back to his. His own narrowed in response. *What did that mean if not an acknowledgement of his claims?* She'd planned to keep this baby secret from him. Blood rushed to his temples in a flush of heat and anger. Just as well she had no way out of this arrangement. She'd never escape him again.

'I...' she flailed. 'You see...'

'I don't see, Philly,' he barged in. 'I don't see at all. You had ample opportunity to tell me you were the woman behind that mask, and yet you said nothing. Then, when we were up at the Gold Coast, I tried to kiss you and you acted like I was mauling you— and yet we'd already made love. What was that all about unless you were wanting to keep that first night a secret?'

She gasped, her eyes wide open in protest. 'You didn't want me that night. It was one thing to make love to some fantasy woman at the ball, but you had no intention of making love to me then. You just didn't want anyone else to. You couldn't stand the thought that anyone else might be interested in me.'

No intention of making love with her? She had to be kidding. He'd burned that night, back in his room, pacing away the tension she'd provoked in his loins.

'No,' he said. 'That doesn't make sense. You wanted to keep your identity secret. That's why you pushed me away that night. So there would be no chance I might recognise my elusive boardroom lover.'

She was shaking her head. 'Things were already too complicated. You wouldn't have believed me.'

'And things are less complicated now? How do you work that out?'

He didn't wait for her answer. He took three strides, stopping at the top of the steps leading down to the thirsty lawn below. 'How do you expect me to believe you?'

'Because it's the truth.'

He sighed, long and deep, before he looked over his shoulder to where she was still standing against the railing. 'So then, explain it to me. Why did you keep that mask on? Why did you run away from me that night, unless it was to ensure I'd never find out who you were? Why didn't you tell me it was you?'

She didn't answer and a train rushed along the track, sounding its horn over the crossing. Then gradually the quiet resumed, leaving only the plaintive notes of the windchimes tinkling in the lame summer breeze.

'Have you forgotten what it was like back then? Forgotten how you were?'

She looked over to him and gave a wan smile. 'Remember the first day I came to your office? When Sam had gone home sick? Remember how you were then?'

'What do you mean?'

'I knew what you thought of me. You'd summed me up and written me off with one glance. I was so low on the food chain I didn't even register.'

'It wasn't like that.'

'Of course it was. There was no way you'd look twice at me. And yet, at the ball...'

'You looked so different that night.'

She gave a shrug, a small laugh. 'You never suspected it was *me*. You never had any plans to make love to plain old Philly Summers. And I didn't want you to find out. Because I knew you wouldn't want to know. It never would have happened if you'd known who I was.'

'That's not true.'

But he knew it was. He hadn't looked twice at her, not the way she was back then. He'd had no idea what was hidden away under that brown suit and those glasses.

'It was such a fantasy, that night,' she continued, her voice low and wistful in remembrance. 'And afterwards, afterwards I got so scared.'

'Scared of what?'

'I couldn't believe what I'd done—what we'd done. I just panicked. I knew you'd resent me for what had happened. I knew you'd be angry. And even if I kept my job, I didn't think I'd ever be able to face you again. I had to get out. So I ran.'

'You thought I'd fire you?'

'I didn't know what you'd do. I had no way of knowing. I just knew you wouldn't be happy to find out that the woman you'd seduced in the boardroom was only me.'

Only me. So she'd hardly been the type of woman that usually attracted him back then. Heck, did she have any idea about how many nights' sleep he'd lost since then thinking about his mystery lover?

And then there'd been the Gold Coast trip. That was when Philly had started to look different. Her clothes, her hair, even getting rid of her glasses. Ever since that trip she'd been a different woman. A sexier woman. And he'd made it plain he thought so in her room that night. And she'd been the one that night to turn him away.

He'd wanted two different women only to find out that they were the same person all along. Surely that counted for something? He wanted to reach out a hand to her then, to soothe her fears and assure her that he did want her, but he wasn't ready to do that. This whole discussion had left more than just a bitter taste in his mouth.

'How long will you wait until you tell your mother about the baby?'

She looked up at him, all hollow eyes and pale skin. 'I thought maybe another month, just to be sure. That should get me over the most critical time.'

'We'll schedule the wedding for a month's time, in that case. We can tell her together then.'

Her head jerked up. 'You still plan on going through with this? You still intend to marry me?'

'You have no choice. Your mother has been told and I certainly don't want to be the one to disappoint her. Do you?'

She dropped her eyes to the decking, her heart hammering in her chest. There was no way in the world she'd do anything to upset her mother—Damien knew that—she'd been effectively locked in this marriage deal from the moment she'd walked through that door.

But if he thought she was trapped, it was nothing to how he was going to feel when he found out the truth.

He was determined to marry her to have control over their child and its upbringing. He had no idea he had control over her heart.

CHAPTER TWELVE

SHE was married. No longer Miss Summers. Now she was Mrs DeLuca, wife to Damien. His ring on her hand, his name in place of hers.

Teringa Park, his country property, had made the perfect setting for their wedding vows. She'd imagined it was just another country home, another executive hobby farm, but she'd been wrong. The lush property dated back to early colonial times, the large home testament to the success and wealth of its first owner.

Just as this wedding was testament to the success and wealth of its current owner.

A large marquee had been set up on the expanse of lawns, which were green and lush in defiance of the dry summer heat. Filmy white fabric had been hung in drifts along the veranda of the old stone homestead and it billowed softly in the gentle breeze, while champagne-coloured helium-filled balloons jostled together in large urns bedecked with ribbons and bows, set about the gardens between bowls of fragrant apricot roses.

The service itself had been brief, though the guest list surprisingly large, considering how few family members there were between them. But obviously Damien wasn't the kind of man who would do anything by halves. The *Who's Who* of Melbourne society was in attendance along with a contingent of society page reporters, and everyone wanted to meet the woman lucky enough to snare Melbourne's most eligible bachelor.

By the end of the day Philly felt drained, emotionally and physically, the stresses and tension of the day overwhelming her. She turned her head to the man at her side, the man to whom her life was now linked, and the magnitude of what she'd done moved through her like an earthquake—a shudder of realisation, an instant of fear as her world shook under her.

She had the perfect husband—rich, intelligent, drop-dead gorgeous. She was the envy of every woman here, if the looks from the assembled guests were any indication. She had everything, or so they thought.

Strange, how empty you could feel, when you were supposed to have everything. Strange how those things everyone seemed to want did nothing to fill the hole deep inside her, the hole that could never be filled with mere luxury and a marriage built on control.

The one bright light was her mother. She sat on a shady terrace watching the proceedings, unable to erase the smile from her face. She looked serene today, even beautiful, in a silky soft aqua outfit Damien himself had personally selected for her and it complemented her pale skin and softly waved regrowing hair perfectly. Make up enhanced her features, already looking healthier than they had in months.

Damien had been right. While news of the baby was sure to delight her mother, knowing that Philly was married and that her grandchild would therefore be raised within a family unit with both parents, would make it all the more special. Already the bloom

on her face made the hastily arranged marriage worthwhile.

But it wasn't just her appearance. It was also the
apparent improvement in her health. Even the doctors
were amazed by the sudden change in her well-being,
the steadying of her condition and the indisputable
easing of the pain. Quite simply, her mother seemed
a different woman.

Philly hugged the thought to her chest. How much
more so would her mother be when she discovered
the whole truth? That she would have a grandchild
again. And now, with her mother's progress, it
seemed more certain every day that she would get to
hold that grandchild.

She watched as Marjorie handed her mother a cool
drink. Damien had even managed to track down the
nurse and retain her as her full-time companion. She
stole a glance up at the man at her side, still confused
by the person he was. For someone who 'didn't do
family', he'd done all he could to make Daphne's life
more comfortable. That would have been enough for
Philly, she couldn't have expected more. Yet beyond
that the two seemed to share an easy relationship, a
genuine relationship, and she could tell there was a
warmth and sincerity from Damien that went further
than mere obligation.

Had he changed? Was there a chance his warmth
would extend to her too? In the past few weeks he'd
been distant, focused on work, while wedding arrangements had been drawn up around him, almost
as if now that she'd agreed to become his wife he had
no further need of her. But was there a chance her
love might one day be reciprocated? Was there a

chance that this marriage might mean more to him than the means of controlling his child's upbringing?

Damien's hand brushed against hers, snaring it in his grip and interrupting her thoughts. She looked up at him.

'Did I tell you how beautiful you look today?'

She felt herself colour under his sudden scrutiny. The ivory silk gown was indeed a triumph of design and needlework, the line complementing her body as it moulded to her shape before spilling into an extravagantly full skirt. It was enough to wear it to feel beautiful. Having Damien tell her it was true was something else entirely.

He squeezed her hand and smiled down at her as the last of the guests drifted away. 'I have something for you,' he said. 'Come with me.'

Dusk was falling, the light changing by the minute as the night inexorably clawed out to claim the day. Marjorie had taken her mother indoors as the summer heat tempered into warm evening and the wind picked up, bringing dark clouds and the promise of a summer storm.

She smiled back at him as he tugged on her hand. 'Come on,' he said.

He led the way around the house, their steps crunching on the white gravel leading to the garage. She frowned. There was a champagne-coloured sports car parked alongside—someone had left their car here, though why anyone would leave a car like that... Hang on, there was something else— It was tied with a wide ribbon and bow.

She looked up at Damien, confused, but he only met her stare with an inscrutably questioning look of his own.

'Do you like it?'

'Do I like it?' He had to be kidding. 'You mean…?' She looked from Damien to the car and back again. 'You mean, it's mine?'

He dipped his head in the briefest affirmation. 'Consider it a wedding gift.'

She thought about her mother's ageing sedan that she used for the shopping and their infrequent trips, as different from this vehicle as a wooden dinghy to a top of the line ski boat. 'I'm not sure I'll be able to handle it.'

'I'll give you lessons. Starting tomorrow.'

He pulled something from his pocket—a loop of satin ribbon tied with a key. He lifted it over her head, placing it around her neck, his hands lingering at her shoulders.

She looked up at him, one hand cradling the key, stunned by his gesture and guilty that she hadn't thought to make him a gift.

'But I have nothing for you.'

He pulled her close, so that his fierce heartbeat was linked to her own but for fine layers of fabric in between. 'I will collect mine…' his head dipped and his mouth brushed over hers—a gentle touch that belied the heat and passion below, the heat she could feel in the look he gave her '…later tonight. But for now, it's time we said goodnight to your mother. It's time she learned our news.'

Daphne was resting in the large Victorian sitting room inside, sipping on a rare sherry. She beamed up at them as they entered the room, the delight on her face further reinforcing in Philly's mind that for her mother's sake at least she had done the right thing today.

'That was a perfect day,' she said as they both leaned down to kiss her. 'Just a beautiful wedding. Thank you for making me so happy.'

Damien smiled. 'We have more news if you're not too tired already.'

She shook her head. 'It's been a long day and I'll need to turn in soon but I don't want it to end just yet. Though I don't know what you could tell me that would top today's excitement.'

He looked across at Philly and nodded, letting her give the news. Philly sat down alongside her mother and took her hands in her own. 'Mum,' she said, watching her mother's face intently. 'This might come as a bit of a surprise, but we're going to have a baby. I'm pregnant.'

Daphne snatched her hands out from between Philly's and slapped them up against her open mouth, her eyes wide with shock.

'Oh!'

A second later tears welled up in those wide eyes until they brimmed over. 'But this is wonderful. Just wonderful.'

Damien leaned closer. 'You're not disappointed? We jumped the gun a bit on the wedding.'

She pulled her hands away, brushing away the tears which were still falling. 'How could I be disappointed? And don't you think I know what it's like to love someone so much you can't wait until the wedding? Remember I was young and in love myself once.'

He would have argued—he knew nothing of love, and love had nothing to do with how their baby had been conceived, but this was no time for argument. Besides, it wasn't as if he didn't feel something for Philly. He wanted her, in bed and out of it, and knowing he had her now, knowing she was tied to him, was more satisfying than he could have imagined.

But that was hardly the same as love...

He watched Daphne's eyes settle on her daughter, suddenly more alive and alight with possibilities than he had ever seen them, before she pulled her into an embrace, Philly laughing out loud with the reception to their news and the delight taken in it by her mother. Laughter merged with tears as they rocked together and, watching them, mother and daughter, his breath caught in his chest as if something had swung free, something hard-edged and heavy, that rammed against his lungs, winding him, before breaking off and plunging deep into his gut.

Philly's eyes landed on his and her smile broadened as their hazel lights shone warm and real into his, setting the space inside him strangely aglow.

He felt a deep satisfaction and a good deal of pride, together with a whole plethora of unfamiliar emotions he couldn't even begin to put a name to.

'I can't believe it,' Daphne said, releasing her daughter from her arms only enough to take her hands in hers. 'Remember that promise you made to me? That you even cared enough to make that promise meant so much but I never once thought it might actually happen.'

'Promise?' Damien shifted, noticing Philly's back stiffen. 'What are you talking about?'

'Oh, that,' Philly replied, shakily trying to laugh it off, her eyes evading his. 'It seems nothing now.'

'Nothing?' said her mother. 'How can it be nothing, when your daughter promises you something you think only a miracle can deliver and yet she makes it happen? It's truly a miracle.'

'What did she promise you?'

'Damien,' said Philly, grabbing his hand. 'Mum looks tired. I'll tell you later.'

'But Philly sounds such a wonderful daughter,' he said, ignoring her attempts to stop him. 'Tell me, Daphne, about how special my new bride is. What did she promise you?'

Daphne patted Damien on the hand, fresh tears pooling in the corners of her eyes.

'Well, it was after Monty, Annelise and baby Thomas died in that terrible accident. I was so upset about the family, and about my grandson. It was so unfair—he was just so young. And I felt cheated. I was a grandmother and yet I'd never had the chance to be one. I never even got to hold him or to kiss his soft cheek or feel his tiny hand cling to my finger...'

Damien reached for her hand then and squeezed it, even though dread was seeping inside him, settling into dank, stagnant pools that banished the sensations of contentment and goodwill he'd been feeling just moments earlier.

She stared ahead, her vacant eyes fixed on a point in the middle distance. 'Not a day goes by that I don't wonder what he would be doing now or how he would be growing. Not a day goes by that I don't feel the pain of his loss.'

She swallowed and turned her face back to Damien's. 'When they discovered my cancer was terminal I thought I'd never have the chance of holding a grandchild at all. But Philadelphia knew what it meant to me. She knew how much I yearned for another grandchild and she made me a promise.'

She blinked rapidly, clearing the tears from her eyes as she took a deep breath. He held his.

'It seems quite mad now yet it meant so much to me at the time—and now? Well, maybe it wasn't so mad, after all. I remember it was my birthday and I was feeling particularly sad and she promised me then that she would do anything she could to make me happy and that I wasn't going anywhere without holding her baby first.'

'She said she would do—*anything*?' He directed the half-statement half-question to Daphne but his eyes were searching for the answer on Philly's face, waiting for her to deny it but knowing by the fear in her swirling hazel eyes that she couldn't.

'Yes.' Daphne chuckled, oblivious to the sudden tension now crackling in the air between the newlyweds. 'I don't know what Philadelphia had in mind. I thought once the wedding with Bryce fell through that there was no chance but then, as luck would have it, you turned up.'

'As luck would have it.'

His voice was icy and flat, a slippery track she felt herself sliding along, further and further away from him.

'And I'm a very lucky woman because of it. But now I must rest. So, if you'll excuse me...'

'I'll see you to your room,' Philly offered, relishing the thought of a moment's respite from the heated accusations of his dark eyes, but Daphne would have none of it.

'No! Marjorie can look after me. It's your wedding night, after all.'

Daphne made her goodnights and disappeared with Marjorie in a whirl of excitement and congratulations. The second they'd left the room Philly turned, trying to take the offensive.

'Damien, it's not how it sounds. We have to talk.'

Without looking at her, he walked straight past and out of the room, leaving her to chase after him in his wake, a combination of his woody cologne, fury and a sense of betrayal wafting behind him. Lifting her full-length silk skirts she tripped down the hallway after him, barely able to keep up with his long, purposeful stride. He entered the room that was to have been theirs, the massive master suite, dominated by the large four-poster bed intended for the newlyweds to share tonight.

But the bed might not have been there for all the notice Damien took of it. He moved straight to the walk-in wardrobe, where he collected a leather overnight case and started flinging the few items he'd brought into it.

'What are you doing?' she asked.

'What does it look like? I'm leaving.'

'Damien, let me explain.'

'Explain what?'

'It's not how it sounds.'

'No? You mean you didn't make that promise to your mother?'

'Yes, I did, but that doesn't mean—'

'You didn't say you'd do anything you could?'

'Damien, that's not the point.'

'Isn't it? You promised to do anything you could to give your mother a grandchild. When it all went belly-up with Bryce you had to find some other way of doing what you'd promised, and quickly. And you found it in me.'

He strode across the room with long, purposeful strides into the large *en suite* bathroom. 'What did your mother say?' he continued, hurling toiletries into the bag. '"As luck would have it, you turned up"'.

'No, Damien, it wasn't like that. I explained all this to you before.'

'Did you? Seems you left out the best bit. You left out the bit about being determined to have a baby. Someone's baby. *Anyone's* baby. That night at the masquerade ball, you weren't there for my benefit. You were trawling for a sperm donor.'

His words cut her deep, so deep that she was unable to respond. It hadn't been like that...

'My God,' he continued, 'when I think that I almost believed you. I thought all you wanted to do was to keep this baby a secret. And, no doubt, you did. Until you worked out there was an even bigger prize. You could have the baby and the money too. Money and luxury for life. Not a bad return for one night's work.'

He lifted his head to look at her. 'Such a wonderful daughter.' He zipped up the bag, shaking his head. 'Such a lousy wife.'

'Damien, it's not true. You have to listen to me. Please.'

'Why should I listen to you? You've lied to me ever since we met. Every step of the way you've hidden the truth, pretending to be something you're not, the shy virgin, the dutiful daughter. Well, the truth is out. You're neither dutiful nor shy. You're manipulative and devious, out for what you can get.'

'I *never* pretended to be anything, least of all a shy virgin. I never said that.'

'No? You didn't have to. Those baggy suits. The big glasses. You looked like a shy little mouse but all the while you were planning with rat cunning.'

'What? Now you're blaming my wardrobe for what's happened? Listen to yourself, Damien. You're not making any sense.'

'Maybe not but at least now I'm seeing sense. I'm seeing things I should have seen a long time ago.'

He tossed the bag over his shoulder and stormed across the room to the door.

'Where are you going?'

'Anywhere you're not.'

'But you can't go, not yet.'

'Why not? You've got what you wanted—the baby, a husband, somewhere your mother will be comfortable and well looked after. You've fulfilled your promise. You have no more need of me.'

'That's not true. I do need you.'

He tossed her a look of disdain over his shoulder as he headed across the driveway to the detached triple garage. 'Why? Have you made more promises you haven't bothered to share with me?'

'No! But I need you, Damien. I... I love you.'

He stopped dead at the garage door, his hand on the automatic door opener and his head lowered as the metal door rolled up and away.

Her breath was fast and shallow, her heart hammering as she waited for his response, any response.

When the door had rolled high enough he stepped under and around to the side of his black BMW, tossed in the bag and finally turned, his features frozen, his eyes cold and hard.

'I'm disappointed, Philly. For a woman who's gone to the lengths you have to get pregnant, I would have expected something much more creative than that. Running out of ideas, are you?'

He lowered himself into the car and turned the key, kicking the black beast into life. She ran to the side of the car as he pulled his door shut, her voice rising to counter the engine.

'Damien, it's the truth. And no matter how much you don't want my love and don't need it, you've got it. And I don't even know why. But it's true. I love you.'

He gunned the motor, one hand on the steering wheel, the other tense over the gear stick as his window slid down in a hum. 'Don't bother, Philly. That's hardly likely to change things, even if I did believe you.'

The window slid up and the car jumped forward out of the garage. Philly sprang back as the sleek car roared out.

'Damien!' But he was gone, in a cloud of rich petrol fumes and the powerful roar of an engine being given its head.

He couldn't go—not like this! He had to believe her. She had to convince him. But how could she do that? She looked around, her eyes falling on the Mercedes coupé still parked just outside the garage, the large gold ribbon still tied around it. She touched the key at her throat, the key Damien had placed there earlier.

He must be heading for the penthouse, intending to spend the night alone there. If she could just talk to him—she needed time to explain, to put his fears to rest, and letting him stew on everything tonight was only going to cement his case against her.

She looked at the car. She hadn't driven it yet and

it was as different from her old sedan as satin was from serge, but it was still only a car. And right now it was her only hope.

She flipped the ribbon necklace over her head as she headed for the car. With two tugs the large bow came away and fluttered to the ground and, collecting her skirts in one hand, she slid behind the wheel, the soft leather seat wrapping itself around her. She took a few seconds to familiarise herself with the controls. Then she snapped on her seat belt and started the engine.

The sports car gave a throaty purr that spelt superb engineering and promised power. She wouldn't need too much of that—she was more interested in making it to the penthouse in one piece than in catching him *en route* after all. With a final deep breath she found the headlights and released the handbrake, easing the car along the driveway.

There was at least twenty kilometres of country road to negotiate before reaching the highway that would take her straight into the city. She couldn't wait to get there.

Thick clouds skudded across the sky, obliterating the moon until the night sky became dark and threatening. Gum leaves and bark danced across the road, whipped along by the rising wind which bowed the roadside trees in the car's powerful headlights.

While the car was smooth and powerful, it was enough to concentrate on the unaccustomed journey and the worsening conditions and she longed for the familiarity of her old sedan. At least on that one she knew which side to find the wipers and indicators in a hurry if she needed.

She missed two turns on the narrow bush roads and

had to backtrack to find the right route, but eventually the glow from the lights over the freeway on-ramp told her she was close. With a sigh of thanks she stretched back into the rich leather upholstery, knowing the worst was over and that the freeway would soon take her into the city and to Damien. The few first drops of rain splatted on to her windscreen. Slowly at first, before fast turning into a torrent.

She almost missed the car on the side of the road as she battled to find the wipers. For a second she thought it was Damien parked there and her heart leapt, but as she got closer she could see the dark colour belonged to a different, older make of car. The bonnet was up and a woman ran out in front of her, waving her arms in the rain. For a second she thought about driving on—it was dark and she wasn't entirely comfortable with the idea of stopping. But the conditions were awful and what if the woman had children in the car? If it was Philly herself who'd broken down the last thing she'd want would be people to just drive by.

If only she'd grabbed her bag before she'd rushed off. At least then she would have had her phone to alert the authorities. As it was, she had no choice…

She pulled up just behind the car and found the button for the window. Cold bullets of rain took advantage of the opening glass, crashing cold and hard on to her face and chest. The woman rushed alongside.

'Can I give you a lift?' Philly asked.

'You can do better than that,' said the woman, pulling open the door before ramming something cold and hard against Philly's cheek. 'You can give me the car.'

CHAPTER THIRTEEN

THE call came at three o'clock in the morning from the security desk downstairs. He hadn't really been sleeping, more like tossing and turning, running over words and conversations in his mind, trying to make sense of the tangle of his thoughts. So the call hadn't really woken him up, but the words the security officer had spoken snapped him immediately to attention.

Two officers. To see him.

He wasn't all that familiar with the workings of the police force but he knew enough to know that they didn't go making social calls at this time of night. He just had time to pull on jeans and a sweater when his doorbell buzzed.

'What's this about?' he said before the uniformed officers had cleared the entrance.

'Mr DeLuca, are you the registered owner of a Mercedes vehicle?' He rattled off a registration number Damien recognised instantly.

'That's my wife's car—yes. I bought it for her as a wedding present. Is there a problem?'

'Can you describe your wife for us, sir?'

'Well, yes. Five-sixish, slim figure, sandy-blonde hair. What's this about?'

The officers exchanged glances. 'You might like to sit down. The car was involved in an accident this evening. I'm afraid we have some bad news.'

His blood ran cold. 'What kind of bad news?'

'The car spun on a bend and went over an embankment. The driver wasn't wearing a seat belt. She was thrown from the car.'

Damien turned away, chilled to the core, trying to swallow though there was nothing to lubricate his throat as the ashes of his past choked him. *'Spun on a bend,' 'Over an embankment'*. Was he truly hearing this or were these images dredged up from another disaster, another tragedy over a lifetime ago?

Why did it seem that history was repeating itself?

'A woman was driving. Do you recognise this?'

The officer placed something in his palm and he tried to concentrate as he looked down on the loops of thin satin ribbon and a key—the same key he'd placed around Philly's neck just last night. His fingers curled tight around the cold metal. 'My wife... Is she badly hurt... Or...?'

'Mr DeLuca,' said one officer, his voice laden with compassion. 'It's more serious than that. The driver was killed. Under the circumstances we fear it may be your wife. We'd like you to come and assist with identifying the body.'

Philly!

They thought it was Philly. But he'd left her back at the house. It couldn't be her. He'd left the car out of the garage. Someone must have stolen it. But then why would they have the key?

There was one way to find out.

He explained and reached for the phone. She had to be at the house. Someone else must have taken the key and stolen the car. That had to be what had happened. He called up the number from the phone's memory, knowing he'd never key it in as quickly while in this state. Eventually his manager answered, businesslike but clearly half-asleep himself.

'It's Damien,' he said. 'I need to know if Mrs DeLuca is in the house. It's important. And check the garage too,' he added as an afterthought.

He found shoes while he waited, avoiding the pity-filled eyes of the policemen as they looked everywhere but at him. But it wasn't Philly. It couldn't be.

Eventually the manager came back, his worried manner immediately sending shivers down Damien's spine. The words only confirmed his tone. No sign of her. Hadn't slept in any of the rooms. And the car was gone.

He held on to the phone for a good minute longer, only half-aware of the concerned voice on the other end of the line. 'Phone me on my mobile immediately if you hear from her,' he said at last, hanging up.

He looked over to the officers, his mind blank, his gut cold and empty. 'Let's go,' he said.

She must have followed him. Why the hell hadn't he considered she might do that? She'd followed him and now she was dead. *Their child was dead.* Grief welled up within him with the force of a tidal wave.

And it was all his fault!

She'd wanted to talk and he'd run. She'd wanted him to stay and he'd fled. She'd told him she loved him and he'd turned his back on her.

And so she'd followed him. Why would she have done that? Why had she been so determined to make him see reason if she already had everything she wanted? Unless the baby and the house weren't enough. Had she really needed him too? Had she really loved him?

She'd crashed, gone over an embankment, had never stood a chance in a car she hadn't known how to handle. A car he'd given to her. He'd inflicted upon her the same fate that had met every other member of his family. He'd done that to her because he'd never once had the courage to accept what she'd said and faced up to what he really felt.

That he needed her. That she made him feel special and strong and protective. That he wanted to look after her.

That he loved her.

Anguish twisted him inside.

My God, but he did!

He loved her. And now it was too late.

He'd never wanted to love. Love only compounded pain, made it infinitely worse than it would otherwise be. But why had he thought he could deny love by simply ignoring its existence, by simply not thinking the thoughts or saying the words?

By not telling the woman he loved?

He was right not to want to love. Wouldn't the pain he was feeling right now be so much easier to bear if he hadn't loved her?

But he hadn't told her, and right now that made his pain worse. He'd denied what she'd meant to him and he'd rejected her love. How must she have felt following him along those roads in those conditions? She must have been desperate to catch up with him.

The police car pulled up outside the hospital, its lights making crazy patterns on the slick roads. The storm had long gone and a strange calm had descended. That was outside at least. His storm had only just begun.

He looked up at the horizontal concrete façade, the

windows lit with a dull glow and the occasional blip of colour from a machine.

He didn't want to go inside. He wanted to deny it now, even though he knew it must be the truth. It was going to be one of the hardest things he'd ever done. But there was something even harder to follow.

How was he going to tell Daphne?

They led him along the long corridors, the atmosphere antiseptic, their bright fluorescent lighting garish and cold in this late hour. Then they made him wait outside a room in the morgue, giving him even more time to think about how he should have done things differently, how he should have told her what she meant to him, how wrong he'd been.

He hadn't been fair to her. He'd bullied her at work, he'd bullied her at the Gold Coast, and he'd bullied her into this wedding. And now there was no chance to tell her he was sorry.

Now it was too late.

They called him inside, into a room where the clinical furniture and fittings faded into bland insignificance, where the cloaked trolley held centre stage. He walked slowly to one side, the policemen close behind, and stopped, wanting to know, not wanting to know, because until he knew for sure, there was always a chance they were wrong, however unlikely that seemed.

'Mr DeLuca?' The attendant's brow was furrowed with concern.

'She was pregnant, you know. Our first child.'

The man's eyes blinked slowly, as if he hadn't wanted to hear that. 'Are you all right, Mr DeLuca?'

He gave a brief nod. 'Ready,' he muttered on a breath that tasted of death and cold ash.

The attendant peeled back the sheet. Damien's heart stopped and he rocked on his heels as he scoured her face. Under the scratches and contusions her features still looked quite lovely considering she'd suffered such a sudden, savage end, her eyes closed, her lips slightly parted as if ready to draw her next soft breath. She looked at peace.

But she didn't look familiar.

'It's not Philly.' He sagged on a breath that brought relief, just as quickly replaced by a savage new fear. He turned to the officers behind him.

'So where's my wife?'

CHAPTER FOURTEEN

IT WAS so cold. Two minutes in the driving rain had been enough to soak her to the skin. Now she was out of the weather but there was no way she could warm up here. She'd found what had to be an old picnic rug that smelt as if it had seen more dogs' breakfasts than picnic lunches, but it was at least something to drag over her shoulders and it helped to break up the otherwise wall-to-wall motor oil smell.

She was cramped, uncomfortable, and had no idea of the time, only that it must be still dark and she was so tired but way too cold to sleep. It hurt to move. It hurt not to move. But what hurt more was that she wouldn't even be missed for hours. Damien was at the apartment, most likely, and at the house no one would question her absence before lunch time.

Every time she'd heard a car approach, she'd banged and yelled till she was hoarse. But no one had heard her and the cars had just kept on driving.

She was stuck here, shivering, until the sun rose. How long until sunrise? But how hot was it expected to be today? Right now the idea of warmth was attractive but how long would it take before she cooked inside here?

They had to find her first. *Damien* had to find her first. Before she died...

Before their baby died.

She hugged her abdomen gently, marginally relieved that right now the discomfort she was feeling down there had more to do with a pressing bladder than a sign that anything was wrong with her pregnancy, and she tried to rock in the cramped, airless space, crooning softly as if calming her tiny child.

How long could she hang on to both her bladder and her sanity? Hopefully long enough.

The police had said they'd contact him as soon as they found her, but if they thought there was any way he could sit and wait by a phone while his wife was missing they had him all wrong. Even if they had reason to wonder.

Tactfully they'd asked why it was that a man who'd just married had spent the night in his apartment in town, while his pregnant wife was left somewhere else.

It wasn't easy to explain—a stupid argument—a misunderstanding. In the light of what had ensued, it all seemed so pointless.

By the time he'd started his own search dawn was lightening the sky, tingeing the few remaining clouds pink in an otherwise grey-blue sky. He set out, confident that if she'd been on the highway someone would have found her by now. She had to be somewhere between the house and the highway.

How the woman had stolen the car, he was too scared to think. The only thing he could hang on to was that she was alive somewhere, alive and waiting to be found. She had to be.

He almost missed the car, only the perfect circles of its tail-lights looking too regular amongst the shrubs along the side of the road. Someone had tried to hide it—why else park it like that?

His heart raced as he pulled up nearby, watching

for any indication that anyone was about, but all he could hear was the morning cries of magpies and crows high up in the trees. Until something thumped and thumped again, dull and repetitive and totally at odds with the sounds of a bush morning and hope sprang wild and unfettered in his chest. He heard a cry, muffled and weak, but he heard it all the same and he rushed to the car.

It had to be.

'Philly,' he yelled, his face up close to the metal. 'Is that you? Can you hear me?'

He wasn't sure if it was a squeal of relief or of delight that he heard in response, but it sure was the best sound he'd ever heard.

She was alive.

He checked the boot but there was no external release mechanism. Without a key he'd need to break it open. Unless… The car was old but there was a chance. He pulled open the driver's side door and sent up a silent prayer of thanks when he saw the boot release lever. He flicked it up and heard the satisfying click as the catch was released.

A fraction of a second later he pulled open the boot lid and scooped her out of the small space, holding her in his arms and hugging her tightly to him.

Her gown was torn and grease-stained, an old rag hung off her shoulders; she smelled more of car and oil than her familiar apricot scent and tears had left tracks down her grimy face but she'd never looked more beautiful to him than right now.

'Philly.' He held her close, his lips brushing her brow as she sobbed gently against him.

'You found me,' she said, her voice shuddering on a sob.

'I was afraid I'd lost you for ever. Are you all right? Did they hurt you?'

'I'm stiff and sore and cold. But I think I'm okay. A woman took the car; she had a gun. She made me get in the boot and then drove it into the bushes.'

She'd had a gun.

Breath hissed through his teeth. What might have happened? What was he thinking, to lead her into danger like this?

He carried her to his car and sat inside with her cradled on his lap to pass on his warmth. He pulled the smelly rag from her shoulders and replaced it with the mohair rug from his car. She snuggled closer, enjoying the warmth both his body and the rug lent as he pulled out his mobile phone and made a quick call to the police.

'How did you find me?' she asked when he'd finished the call.

'The police found your car. You weren't in it.' He didn't tell her about the driver; there were some things that could wait. And some things that were more important and couldn't.

'I'm so sorry,' she said, her voice quivering. 'I didn't mean to cause you so much fuss.'

'Shh,' he said. 'It's not your fault. I shouldn't have left like that. You were following me, weren't you?'

'I had to talk to you. You wouldn't believe me. I couldn't let you go, thinking what you did.'

He smoothed her tangled hair with his fingers. 'I was wrong to think all those things. I was wrong.'

'But Damien—' she sniffed, rubbing her nose with her hand '—in a way you were right.'

'No,' he said, interrupting her. 'You don't have to do this now.'

'Please, I have to. I was crazy with wanting a baby; that much was right. I'd asked about IVF but they wouldn't take me on because I wasn't married. I'd even thought about picking someone up, a one-night stand.'

He stiffened, not sure he wanted to hear this.

She looked up at him, her eyes earnest. 'I thought about it but I couldn't do it. I'd all but given up hope of having a baby by the time the masquerade ball happened and it didn't even occur to me that night. Because of you. You made me feel so good, you felt so wonderful, that nothing else mattered. It was only afterwards that I realised what we'd done. I panicked.'

'You really thought I would have sacked you?'

'I didn't know and I was too scared to find out. But as soon as I discovered I was pregnant, I knew you had to be told. I couldn't keep it a secret any longer. I'm sorry now I even waited that long. It made it harder for you to believe me.'

He sighed and squeezed her tight against him. '*I* made it hard to believe you. I didn't want to be close to anyone. But I couldn't stop wanting you. Not believing you became my way of pushing you away. If I couldn't trust you, I couldn't feel anything for you.

'But I was mad,' he said, cocking his ear to the wail of an approaching siren. 'Mad to think I could shut you out. It was only when I thought I'd lost you that I realised just how much you meant to me.'

She looked up at him, her expression hopeful. 'I do?'

He raised her in his lap and brushed his lips against hers. 'Oh, you do.' His lips moved over hers and he felt the tremor that passed through her and the depth it added to her kiss. 'Did I tell you lately,' he said, raising his lips just a fraction, 'that I love you?'

This time she pulled her mouth away completely, her tired eyes blinking, bright and beautiful. 'You've never told me that.'

'Then it's time I did. I love you, Philly. It took almost losing you to realise that, but I do. I love you and I'm proud, even honoured, that you are now part of my family and you will be part of my family for ever, if you still want me after all I've done to you.'

Her eyes shone up at him, her teeth gripping her bottom lip. Tears welled in her bright eyes, as if she was afraid to believe what he was saying.

'Oh, Damien,' she managed to say when the bubble of happiness had cleared from her throat enough to speak. 'I love you so much. I can't imagine being anywhere else. You saved my life.'

'Fair payback,' he said. 'You've given me back mine.'

She opened her mouth as if to argue the point and he shushed her with a finger to her lips as the sirens screamed closer.

'Don't argue with me; any minute now we're going to be surrounded by emergency services and I have much more important things right now to be doing with my time.' And she smiled under his finger, her eyes sparkling as he slanted his mouth over hers, his lips warm and gentle, his breath and his final words moving her soul.

'Much more important…'

EPILOGUE

WHAT a day! Damien turned off the highway, loosening his tie as the hot air blew through the open top. He could have kept on the roof and the air conditioner—the temperature sure warranted it—but now that he was out of the city he wanted to feel the air around him, he wanted to smell the scents of the baking, crisp countryside, he wanted to feel a part of it.

It was a great day—two o'clock in the afternoon and he'd decided that being home was more important than being in the office.

He'd been making a habit of that lately, Enid had been quick to point out. Not that she minded; she'd scolded him half-heartedly as she'd set about rejigging his timetable. He'd spent much of the last two years taking the time to feel things and the novelty was yet to wear off. He'd never have believed he could have found satisfaction in a life outside the office, but then it was only just over two years ago that he'd met Philly and she'd changed everything.

He looked at the clock on the dashboard as he pulled into the driveway. Great, it was still early enough to see little Anna before she went down for her afternoon nap.

He found the women sitting out on the veranda, shaded from the sun and where the breeze cooled naturally as it filtered through the hanging wisteria covering the pergola alongside. A small paddling pool sat between them, a dark-haired toddler sitting within an inflatable safety seat inside, splashing at the shallow water with obvious delight.

She squealed as soon as she saw him round the corner of the home, raising her chubby arms high and calling 'da-da, da-da' in her sweet baby voice. She bounced up and down in the seat, her toothy smile stretching wide across her chubby cheeks.

He swept her up, naked and wet, and she shrieked with delight as he blew raspberries over her skin.

'You're home early,' said Philly, laughing as he reached down to kiss her, the giggling infant still in his arms and replying with raspberries of her own.

'How could I stay away, knowing how much fun the three most important women in my life are having?'

He ruffled the curly black locks of his daughter's hair as she yawned widely, her eyelids suddenly droopy. 'Is it sleep time for you, little lady?'

'I'll take her,' said Daphne, looking slim but healthy in a cool sundress. 'I could do with an afternoon siesta myself.'

She wrapped the infant in a fluffy towel and let her kiss both her parents and wave goodbye wearily before she turned into the house. Damien watched her go before he pulled Philly to her feet and walked with her to the veranda railing.

'It's remarkable, the change in your mother. She could never have been strong enough to lift a child before.'

'I know,' said Philly. 'The doctors are amazed. I know she's far from being out of the woods, but they say it's because she's had a change of attitude; she's allowing the drugs to work.'

Something in her tone twigged in his mind. 'And what do you say?'

She turned from the view to face him. 'I say it's a miracle and that miracle has a lot to do with you and what you've done for my family.'

'You're my family now,' he said, gently lifting her chin. 'Always and for ever. And I thank the stars for the day you walked into my life. I love you, Philly.'

His lips brushed over hers even as she said the words, 'I love you, too.' She caught his intake of air before his kiss deepened, as if powered by the words she'd spoken. When at last he pulled his mouth away, he smiled and reached a hand down to the firm swell of her abdomen.

'And what of our other miracle? How does my son progress?'

She laughed. 'You're so sure he's a boy. Well, maybe you're right, the way this baby is kicking. I think he's practising for when he's the boss. He's going to be just like his dad.'

He wrapped his arms more tightly around her, pulling her close. 'I hope you're not mocking me,' he warned. 'To think I once thought of you as a shy little mouse. You know I'll make you pay for any insubordination.'

'And just what did you have in mind for my punishment?'

His eyes twinkled down at her, the love within them aflame with desire.

'Slow, delicious torture,' he said, tugging her towards the house, his lips curled into a wicked smile. 'I'll have you screaming for release.'

And he did.

*Your dream ticket to
the love affair of a lifetime!*

*Where irresistible men and sophisticated women
surrender to seduction under the golden sun*

**Don't miss this opportunity to experience
glamorous lifestyles and exotic settings in:**

Fiona Hood-Stewart's

AT THE FRENCH BARON'S BIDDING
on sale September 2005, #2490

When Natasha de Saugure was summoned to France by her
estranged grandmother, inheriting a grand estate was the last thing
on her mind—but her new neighbor, Baron Raoul d'Argentan,
believed otherwise. His family had been feuding with Natasha's for
centuries—and the baron didn't forgive....

Seduction and Passion Guaranteed!
www.eHarlequin.com

HPATFBB

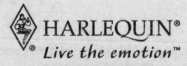

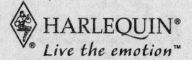

Coming Next Month

HARLEQUIN *Presents*

THE BEST HAS JUST GOTTEN BETTER!

#2487 THE RAMIREZ BRIDE Emma Darcy
Nick Ramirez has fame, fortune—and any girl he wants! But now he's forced to abandon his pursuit of pleasure to meet his long-lost brothers. He must find a wife and produce an heir within a year. And there's only one woman he'd choose to be the Ramirez bride....

#2488 EXPOSED: THE SHEIKH'S MISTRESS Sharon Kendrick
As the ruler of a desert kingdom, Sheikh Hashim Al Aswad must marry a respectable woman. He previously left Sienna Baker when her past was exposed—and he saw the photos to prove it! But with passion this hot, can he keep away from her...?

#2489 THE TYCOON'S TROPHY WIFE Miranda Lee
Reece knew Alanna would make the perfect trophy wife! Stunning and sophisticated, she wanted a marriage of convenience. But suddenly their life together was turned upside down when Reece discovered that his wife had a dark past....

#2490 AT THE FRENCH BARON'S BIDDING Fiona Hood-Stewart
When Natasha de Saugure was summoned to France by her grandmother, inheriting a grand estate was the last thing on her mind—but her powerful new neighbor, Baron Raoul d'Argentan, believed otherwise. His family had been feuding with Natasha's for centuries—and the Baron didn't forgive....

#2491 THE ITALIAN'S MARRIAGE DEMAND Diana Hamilton
Millionaire Ettore Severini was ready to marry until he learned that Sophie Lang was a scheming thief! Now when he sees her again, Sophie is living in poverty with a baby.... Ettore has never managed to forget her, and marriage will bring him his son, revenge and Sophie at his mercy!

#2492 THE TWELVE-MONTH MISTRESS Kate Walker
Joaquin Alcolar has a rule—never to keep a mistress for more than a year! Cassie's time is nearly up.... But then an accident leaves Joaquin with amnesia. Does this mean Cassie is back where she started—in Joaquin's bed, with the clock started once more...?